ANGRY BELLOW

A clearing opened in front of them. Llanga paused on the edge of it, peering through the semi-darkness, head on one side, as he listened for the slightest sound.

Brandon, tense at his side, his heavy-bore rifle gripped firmly in his hands, waited breathlessly.

Suddenly, from the monstrous shadow of a clump of dense **mchwili** trees on the far side of the clearing, they heard a rumbling grunt and a flapping sound. An instant later the mighty bulk of a great bull elephant broke cover and came towards them at a fast run, trunk raised, ears spread wide.

Llanga uttered a gasp. Brandon dropped to one knee and brought his rifle up at the same time. The big bull came on till it was no more than fifteen yards from him, bellowing angrily as it thundered over the ground.

Brandon held his fire till the last possible moment. He felt, rather than saw, Llanga dart away, for cover …

REX BRANDON
JUNGLE HUNTER

WHITE GOLD

by

DENIS HUGHES

Published through
arrangement with
Cosmos Literary Agency

The *Rex Brandon: White Hunter* stories are works of their time. Occasionally, certain outdated ethnic characterizations or slang appear, which contemporary readers may find objectionable. To preserve the integrity of the author's words, these obsolete aspects have remained in place for this edition. The text is presented as it originally appeared.

Editor: Philip Harbottle, Cosmos Literary Agency

Book & Cover design: Rich Harvey, Bold Venture Press

Bold Venture Press, April 2024.
Available in paperback and electronic editions.
Published through arrangement with Cosmos Literary Agency.

©1951 by Denis Hughes;

© 2024 by the Estate of Denis Hughes. All rights reserved.

Originally published in 1951 by Curtis Warren, LTD.

This is a work of fiction. Though some characters and locales may have their basis in history, the events and characters depicted herein are fictitious.

No part of this book may be reproduced without written permission from Cosmos Literary Agency or the publisher.

WHITE GOLD

1

ELEPHANT GRAVEYARD

THE long spacious bar of the Hotel Rhodian was packed to capacity when Rex Brandon sauntered in and glanced round with a casual air that was wholly deceptive. His keen eyes missed no one in the crowd, and few of the faces he saw would be forgotten. It was a habit with this tall bronzed man that he made a mental note of everyone who crossed his devious path through life, and even if he never had occasion to speak with another man he would know that man again once he had seen his face or remembered some insignificant mannerism about him.

Straight-backed as an arrow, with a physique of a modern Sampson, Brandon made an impressive figure in the suit of immaculate white ducks he wore as he strode forward from the door and made his way towards the bar. Expert geologist, world-famous big-game hunter, this man was known and respected in every corner of the earth.

But Brandon was not after game of any kind at the moment. He was enjoying a well-earned vacation in Bulawayo after what had been a particularly strenuous safari into the hinterland of Northern Rhodesia in search of certain mineral deposits. Now he was relaxing, staying at the Hotel Rhodian, dining and sleeping in comfort, toying with the idea of making his next trip a purely pleasure affair.

Rumours of a large herd of elephant had reached his ears. The beasts were reputed to be down in the Limpopo River; or at any rate working the valleys of that mighty river's many tributaries where the feeding grounds were good. To Brandon there was something almost irresistible in the thought of elephant. He had been after them on many occasions in the past, and would certainly do so in the future. The fact that he was within striking distance of their ground was an added incentive when he thought about plans for his next safari. He was even then playing with the idea as he reached the bar and caught the eye of one of the waiters. The grinning man recognised him immediately as an old friend and customer.

Greetings were exchanged while Brandon was served with a long glass of ice-cold beer. The intense heat of the day was wearing off with the fall of evening. From his bedroom window he had seen one of the finest African sunsets of his life. There was a glow of pleasure and peace inside him as he sipped his drink and studied his immediate neighbours.

The man next to him at the bar was a red-faced individual in heat-crumpled clothes. His head was bald and he was sweating freely, despite the constant motion of the electric fan almost directly over his head. Brandon noticed that his hands were broad and thick, immensely powerful. He was probably a planter in town from the outback for a few days' break, he thought. There was that sort of set about him.

At the moment the bald man was staring gloomily into a half-empty glass, listening with half an ear to the swift chatter of a small, sleek-looking man on his other side.

Brandon could not help but overhearing what was being said.

"But I tell you, Meyrick, you won't find a better man for the job than I am!" insisted the little one. "There isn't a hunter north of Capetown with a reputation I've got! And I'm offering my services for a ridiculously small share in the deal."

The bald man, whose name appeared to be Meyrick, turned his head slowly and studied his companion thoughtfully. He did not speak for several seconds. All around them the buzz of conversation went on in the sultry heat of the Rhodian Bar. Rex Brandon found himself listening for Meyrick to speak. It was none of his business, and he made no effort to embroil himself in another man's affairs, but for all that he was conscious of interest.

Meyrick drew a red and white handkerchief from his pocket and mopped his brow, still staring morosely at his sleek-looking companion. Then:

"Now, look here, Chartris," he said in a heavy tone, "I don't want to be rude to you, my friend, but I don't want you with me in any deal I undertake." He spread his podgy hand and waved it vaguely towards Chartris. "You may be a good man with a gun, and you may know Rhodesia like the back of your hand, but if you offered to come along on this show for nothing at all I'd turn you down. Thanks very much, but there it is."

Chartris let his dark eyes rest on Meyrick's face for a moment. There was a great deal of animosity in his gaze. It revealed itself, too, in the tightened corners of his small mouth and little pinched-in lines at the sides of his nose. Chartris was keeping his temper, but it was a case of touch and go for a time. At length he shrugged. His face broke into a smile that carried little humour.

"That's all right by me," he said quietly. "You go and look for your white gold, Meyrick. You may be lucky, but it won't worry me one way or the other." He paused. "Good hunting!"

Meyrick nodded briefly, saying nothing. There was nothing he wished to say at the moment. He was glad when Chartris turned on his heel and elbowed his way towards the swinging doors of the bar.

Rex Brandon smiled quietly to himself as he watched the little drama. This would not be the first time he had seen white hunters trying to sell their services to another man. He knew from experience that many of them were doubtful types; but on the other hand it was easy enough to pick up a really experienced and sound character as a companion for a hunting safari.

Meyrick turned his head and caught Brandon's glance.

Brandon gave a faint grin, nodding slightly. He did not know Meyrick, but liked the look of him. There was a bluntness about the man, and a ruggedness in his appearance that appealed to Brandon. Despite Meyrick's sweating face and well-covered body, there was a determination in his general attitude and manner.

Meyrick poured himself a fresh drink from the bottle that stood on the counter in front of him. He cocked an eyebrow at Brandon and returned his grin.

"What brings you to this dump?" he inquired affably.

"First vacation I've had in quite a time," answered Rex. "I was working in the outback, checking mineral deposits for the Government. Nearest place with civilisation on sale was this, so I drifted here the moment I was through."

Meyrick raised his shoulders and let them sag again.

"Geologist, eh?" he murmured. "You don't look the part, if I may say so."

Brandon grinned. "That's not my fault!" he replied. "Have a drink?"

Meyrick considered for a moment or two, eyed his own bottle thoughtfully. Then he nodded.

"Mighty civil of you," he said. "My name's Meyrick, Randolph Meyrick. Randy, for short."

"I'm Brandon," replied the other.

Meyrick's face showed an increase of interest. "Rex Brandon?" he asked. "Maybe this is my lucky day after all. Not that I thought it was a little while ago."

Brandon smiled enigmatically. "Good health," he said, raising his glass. "What's on your mind, Meyrick?"

"Plenty, but I don't intend to blab about it here." He glanced round the crowded bar. More and more people were coming in now. There was barely room to stand, and every table in the place was occupied. Even the floor-space at the bar itself was at a premium.

Brandon lowered his voice: "Pardon me mentioning it," he said apologetically, "but I couldn't help overhearing the conversation you were having with that fellow Chartris. I admire your reading of character. He wouldn't be an ideal man to take along on a hunting trip, I should say."

Meyrick shot him a swift glance. "Wouldn't have had him at any price!" he grunted. "I didn't ask him to nose in on my affairs; he invited himself when he picked up a rumour that I needed a reliable man."

"Hunting trip?" inquired Brandon idly.

"Sort of," agreed Meyrick. His tone was a trifle guarded as if he did not intend to give too much away at the moment. Brandon decided he would probably learn all about it in a little while. He was in no hurry;

and being on holiday, the idea of Meyrick's hunting trip gave him something to think about.

"Have some food with me," he offered.

Meyrick mopped his face again. He looked at Brandon searchingly for an instant, then nodded firmly, grinning as he did so.

"Good idea!" He paused, taking another drink. Then: "I might have a proposition to interest you, Brandon," he added.

"Always ready to listen," murmured Brandon. He looked round the bar as he spoke. There was now no sign of the sleek-looking Chartris. He had apparently given Meyrick up as a bad job and gone completely. Brandon forgot all about the man.

He and Meyrick had a few more drinks, by which time they were both of them ready for a meal. In the luxury of the dining room of the Hotel Rhodian, the two of them ate and talked, friendship growing as the minutes passed. But Meyrick was a cagey man. He did not open up to Brandon on the subject of his hunting trip until the liqueur stage of the meal.

Sipping brandy, Meyrick studied his companion closely.

Brandon guessed that he was making up his mind before embarking on what would amount to an offer. He was very interested, especially in view of the remark Chartris had made regarding "white gold," that magic term which stood for ivory. A lot would depend on whether the proposed trip fitted in with Brandon's own movements.

Brandon caught himself up and grinned. Here he was already deciding if he would accept Meyrick's offer or not, and he had not even been asked as yet!

"Stumbled on something that would have interested you a little while ago," said Meyrick quietly. "The geologist in you, I mean."

Brandon met his gaze, raising his eyebrows inquiringly.

"Yes," he murmured. "Tell me about it."

Meyrick leant forward, elbows on the table. He looked down at his brandy glass and twirled the stem between his thick fingers.

"Curious strata rock formation in the Matan Hills," he said. "You fellows would know what it is, of course, but I'd never seen anything like it before. It certainly had me guessing!"

Brandon felt the pulses beating faster in his brain. If Meyrick was baiting his offer with geological attractions so much the better; but he did not think Meyrick could pull any unknown rock formation out of the hat so simply as that.

"Can you describe this strata?" he asked in an unhurried tone. "I'm always intrigued by anything of that kind."

Meyrick smiled faintly. "Now you're asking something, my friend!" he said. "The best I can do is to tell you it was an iron coloured rock with thick streaks of purply red stuff running through it at a sharp angle." He grinned. "Does that convey anything to you?"

Brandon nodded. "Strataed ferrous," he murmured. "Not so particularly uncommon as you might expect, but it's interesting stuff. I've been hunting for examples bearing a chromic streak for years, but I've never struck any yet."

"What would that be like?" inquired Meyrick.

"It's more or less the same as you described, but there are thousands of tiny greenish flecks in the purple red streak of the faulting."

Meyrick sat up straight as if someone had jammed a pin in his back.

"Green flecks!" he blurted out. "Good heavens, man, I forgot to mention that. There are green flecks in the strata! Does that make it chromic-ferrous?"

Brandon was silent for a full thirty seconds before he answered. "Yes," he said quietly. "It's very rare and almost as valuable as pure gold when you find it."

Meyrick said nothing for a moment. Then: "Look here, Brandon, I know you're a busy man; but I also know you're a first-class hunter as well as a geologist. If you like the idea you can combine business and pleasure." He put his head on one side slightly, watching Brandon with an oddly bird-like expression. "Profitable pleasure, too, if the notion appeals to you."

Brandon refused to allow himself to seem too eager, but he knew now that he was committed. With the prospect of a hunting safari after elephant combined with a prospecting trip to investigate the chromic-ferrous formation, there could be no turning it down.

"Let's have a few more details," he said with a smile. "I have time on my hands at the moment, but you must realise that I can't just wander off into the blue for an indefinite period. How long do you anticipate being away?"

"Two or three months, I suppose. It's rather hard to tell exactly, because one never quite knows what will crop up. You know that as well as I do, of course."

Brandon nodded agreement. "True," he said. "But as long as I have a general idea that's all I want."

Meyrick grunted and grinned. "Call it a couple of months and you won't be far out," he said with a chuckle. "Now then, are you interested in elephants and their habits?"

"I certainly am," agreed Brandon quickly. "Is that what you're after? I've been hearing rumours of a large herd down on the Limpopo; but you mentioned the Matan Hills when you spoke of the rock formation. The two don't add up, do they?"

Meyrick took his time in answering. Then: "I'm not after the herd down there," he said. "I expect you've heard tales of elephant graveyards, haven't you?"

"Everyone has, but I doubt if they really exist. Nobody has ever found one. There'd be a fortune in ivory for the man who located one."

Meyrick's eyes sparkled for an instant, then he leant forward intently, his face less than six inches away from Brandon's.

"In that case I'm a wealthy man!" he said. "You can be rich as well, if you throw in your lot with me on the deal. What do you say, Brandon?"

Brandon grinned despite himself. "It isn't so much the profit I'm after," he said. "But do you really mean to tell me that you've actually located one of these fabulous elephants' graveyards? I can hardly believe it!"

Meyrick thrust his chin out almost belligerently.

"I've found it all right!" he said. "But I'm not a big-game hunter and I don't know enough about the white gold racket to handle this thing on my own. Will you come in on the deal? There's a share of the ivory and the chance to investigate your precious chromic-ferrous strata formation."

Brandon rubbed his hand across his face, glancing round the dining room of the hotel with canny eyes.

"It's an excellent notion," he mused. "How did you come to find this graveyard?"

"Stumbled on it by chance when I was on a short safari from my plantation," answered Meyrick. "It may sound odd, but I didn't realise at the time what I'd come across. I'm not a hunting man myself, but was following some lion spoor with one bearer. We found the lion all right, a big brute that charged almost as soon as we sighted it. My man was killed before I got the lion. Then I nosed round a bit and found this deep depression full of scrub and suchlike. It was littered with elephant skeletons and tusks. Dozens and dozens of them." He broke off, thinking deeply.

"This is in the Matan Hills?" queried Brandon quietly.

Meyrick nodded his big bald head. "Sure," he said. "I've been telling you, haven't I? What I need is a first-class big-game hunter to come in with me on the deal. This is something I don't know much about, if you understand. I've got to have someone entirely reliable with me; and I think you're my man."

"Have you got the men and equipment for a full-scale safari?" asked Brandon, slowly.

Meyrick nodded. "Everything's fixed," he said. "All that remains is for you to say you'll come along with me. We can be away from here tomorrow morning. Reach my place in little more than a day. Get the safari fixed and move off. Nothing to it. This graveyard, or whatever you'd call it, is less than a fortnight's trek from the door."

Brandon didn't waste any more time in deliberating as to whether he would go with Meyrick or not; he'd already made up his mind, anyway. An elephants' graveyard and some rare rock formations were sufficient incentive.

"We'll start tomorrow, Meyrick!" he said, thrusting out his hand across the table and finding it gripped firmly by the bald man.

"Good," replied his companion. "I knew I could rely on you. A man with your reputation couldn't possibly turn his back on an opportunity of this kind!"

Brandon glanced round. He wondered if Meyrick, in his innocence, had let the word get round that he had found such a thing as a white gold hoard in the Matan Hills. It would be better if he had not.

"Did Chartris know what you'd located?" he asked keenly.

Meyrick shook his head. "I don't think so," he said. "I didn't tell him, but it's possible that he might have picked up a rumour or a hint from somewhere. Things have a knack of getting around in this darned country!" He pulled a wry face, and grinned. "Why, I can remember—"

But Brandon was no longer listening.

He jumped up from the table and whirled round, leaving Meyrick with his mouth half-open and a look of blank surprise on his heavy features.

Somewhere over Brandon's right shoulder as he had been sitting he had caught a faint sound above the murmur of noise in the dining room. Now he realised for the first time that there was another table almost concealed from his view by a stone column and a potted fern of some sort. It was while he was listening to Meyrick that some sixth sense had warned him that their conversation was being picked up by a man at the partly-concealed table.

Snaking round swiftly, he stepped across and glared at the man. With only three or four feet between tables it would have been a simple matter for the man to hear what was said. Brandon cursed himself for a fool. He should never have allowed Meyrick to talk so freely in a public place.

The man at the table looked back at him with a mixture of surprise and hostility.

"What's bitten you?" he demanded suddenly, recovering.

"Nothing," answered Brandon, curtly. "I apologise for intruding. Thought you were someone else." He turned, sitting down with Meyrick again, remembering the face of the man who'd been listening. It was the face of a bad-hat, if ever there was one. A thoroughly untrustworthy specimen, thought Brandon grimly. Meyrick said nothing, but watched him thoughtfully. Brandon sat half swivelled round in his chair, one eye on the concealed table and the man who sat there. A few moments later the man got to his feet and stalked out of the room with a venomous glare in Brandon's direction.

"He was listening to us," said Brandon. "Ever seen him before?"

Meyrick shook his head. "No," he admitted.

"Are you staying in this hotel?" asked Brandon

Again Meyrick nodded. "Room 14," he volunteered.

"I'll meet you there later," answered Brandon. "Just at the moment I think it would be a wise move to find out what our friend is up to and who he is. There's the stamp of the veldt about him. Probably a hunter—like Chartris. He may be up to something; on the other hand, I may be all wrong. See you presently, Meyrick. The deal's on, by the way!"

The restaurant was busy, so that Brandon had no great difficulty in picking his way unobserved to the door in the wake of the stranger. That the man was an eavesdropper, he was positive. The question in Brandon's mind was whether or not he was a lone wolf. If he wasn't, there were all manner of possibilities that could crop up in the future. He was not far behind the man when they left the hotel.

2

TANGLED INTRIGUE

WHEN Brandon left the Hotel Rhodian the street outside was dark. Crowds of people passed to and fro; cars purred by in both directions. The night life of Bulawayo was starting. It would never be hectic, but it passed for such in Africa

Brandon paused for an instant on the raised step of the hotel building and looked up and down the road. Shop windows were brightly illuminated; the air smelt of flowers, human sweat, animals and petrol fumes. It was an atmosphere that was almost oriental, save that here the majority of the people were dark skinned..

He spied his quarry walking swiftly down the side of the street, looking neither to right nor left.

Brandon started in his wake, more intent on seeing where the man went than on any other count. He wondered who he was and what he was doing here. With any luck he would be able to answer those questions before long, he told himself. In the meantime, watchfulness was obviously the line to take.

Whether his quarry knew he was being tailed or not there was no way of telling, but before many minutes were up the man succeeded in giving Brandon the slip.

It happened when the two of them turned off the main street they were using. The stranger, who was tall, thin and angular, with iron-grey hair and a hatchet face, quickened his stride. Brandon did likewise. His quarry was twenty or thirty yards in the lead when he reached a standing taxi-cab, a decrepit vehicle with a wheezy engine, that was idling noisily.

To his disgust Brandon saw the man glance over his shoulder as he drew level with the taxi. Next moment he was jumping in and saying something to the driver. Brandon broke into a run, but the taxi was already moving before he had covered half the distance. There was not enough light at that point to get the number of the car, but it struck Brandon that the entire thing had been so slickly arranged that the taxi must have been waiting for its passenger. If that was true, it was clear that Meyrick and he had been under observation ever since they met in the Hotel Rhodian.

Brandon stood on the street for a moment as the winking tail light of the taxi disappeared. He muttered something beneath his breath, then shrugged and turned back the way he had come. There was no sense in hanging around now. He might as well return to the hotel and see what Meyrick was up to, he decided.

As he walked he wondered if the tall, thin stranger had any connection with Chartris, the unwanted hunter Meyrick had sent about his business. It was certainly a possibility to bear in mind.

Back at the hotel he ran Meyrick to earth in the bar.

"What did you discover?" he asked, as he ordered a drink for Brandon. "Is the fellow spying on us?"

Brandon grinned. "I should think it's a dead cert!" he replied. "But I lost him before I could find out much. Now I'm wondering if the waiter in the restaurant couldn't give us a little information. Hang on here while I go and see."

Meyrick nodded without speaking. He took the whole thing with a wonderful casualness that amazed Brandon. It made him feel as if he was acting like a schoolboy; yet his needle-sharp instinct warned him that this was not the case. There was trouble ahead if they were not extra careful. It could come from a dozen different sources. From Chartris; from the thin stranger; from the wilds themselves.

Brandon found the waiter who had served the stranger. The man was a sharp-witted Kaffir, with bright beady eyes and a nose for any extra coin on the side.

"You served a man at this table not long ago," said Brandon quietly. "He is well known, isn't he? I'll pay you well if you tell me who he is and what he is doing in this town. Tell me anything you can about him."

As smart and efficient as any West-End waiter, the man ducked his head knowingly.

"The bwana asks much," he replied with a grin. "But I tell you something."

"Go ahead." Brandon rattled some coins in his trousers pocket. He put a lot of meaning into the action. The waiter had no difficulty in catching on speedily.

"They call him Darracq," he informed his customer. "He was a big elephant hunter not long back, but now he is nothing. The government will not permit him to hunt, for he broke certain laws."

Brandon pursed his lips thoughtfully. "Lost his licence, did he?" he murmured. "And his name's Darracq…? I seem to remember hearing something about the business. He killed a native woman in a kraal up-country, didn't he?"

"That is so," replied the waiter. "Now I do not know what he does, or why he is here, but he is not a good man, bwana. It is said that there are many who would like to see him dead; but I do not know. I dwell in the city now, and am out of touch with a lot of my people."

Brandon regarded the Kaffir with a faint grin. There was something proud in the way he held himself, and his white uniform might have been a military rig-out by his bearing.

"You served in the army, didn't you?" he said.

The other nodded briskly. "Yes, that is why I am friend of the white man—if he is good man."

"Thanks a lot for the information," murmured Brandon. Money changed hands. "Don't say a word of this to anyone."

The man nodded understandingly. "My wishes go with you, bwana," he whispered.

Brandon returned to the bar and joined Meyrick. He told him what he had learnt.

"It's obvious, isn't it?" he said. "Darracq, I should say, is working with someone else. They've picked up news of your white gold find and mean to muscle in on the deal. You mark my works, Meyrick, we'll be watched and followed all the time from now after what Darracq heard us saying in the dining room."

Meyrick shrugged.

"You don't seem very worried about the idea," grinned Brandon.

"Why should I be?" countered Meyrick. "No one knows exactly where this place is, but me. So long as we are forewarned, we shan't stick our necks out; and no one will try to harm us until they know where the stuff lies hidden. We can look after ourselves if it comes to the pinch."

Brandon warmed considerably to Meyrick for the sentiments he expressed. There was something very devil-may-care in the make-up of his companion and partner.

"That's the idea!" he said, heartily. "Now I suggest we retire to my room and discuss the details."

"Suits me down to the ground," agreed Meyrick.

When Darracq left the Hotel Rhodian he was angry with himself and with Brandon for spoiling his chance of hearing even more exact details than he had so far gleaned. It had been through Chartris that Darracq first heard whisper of the possibility that Meyrick—whom he considered a fool—had stumbled on an elephants' graveyard, it was a widely-held belief that there were such places where old elephants went to die when they felt their days were drawing to a close, but no man had ever found such a place. However, Chartris had been positive from Meyrick's manner that the man had done what no one else had succeeded in doing—and by sheer chance. Rumours get round, and Chartris had picked this one up in a barroom chat over Kaffir beer. Meyrick's own workers on his plantation seemed to know things; hence the interest shown by Chartris in trying to get the job of acting as hunter to Meyrick on safari.

Chartris had failed, but Darracq used more subtle methods to find out what he wanted to know. It had been remarkably speedy work on his part to listen in on Meyrick and Brandon, and now he was taking his information to someone who could back it with the necessary funds to equip and prepare a party for the coming safari.

If Meyrick and Brandon meant to go after elephant, dead or alive, or both, Darracq was equally intent on following them.

The taxi dropped him at another hotel in town. He paid off the driver and went inside, straight up to a suite of rooms. Without bothering to knock, he entered, glanced round and smiled thinly as a man of about fifty rose to his feet with an impatient gesture.

"Why don't you learn the ordinary manners of a decent person?" he demanded. "Isn't it usual to knock before you walk into private rooms?"

"Pipe down, Grier!" sneered Darracq, tossing his hat on to a chair and peering round. "Don't forget that you do what I tell you to when it suits me! Where's Pierrette?"

Grier hesitated for a moment. His eyes were weak and avoided Darracq. There was weakness in every line of the man's face; and it was obvious that he was not only under the domination of Darracq, but afraid of him.

"She has a headache," he said, at length. "Gone to bed early. There isn't any need to disturb her."

Darracq laughed nastily. "There would be if I felt that way inclined," he snapped. "I don't, so keep your hair on! That girl will crawl to me when I'm good and ready for her. Right now, I can afford to wait."

Grier drew a deep breath of frustration. "Someone will murder you one day," he said in a nervous whisper.

Again Darracq laughed, this time softly. "It won't be you!" he said, tauntingly. "You haven't got the guts, for one thing, and if I were to die the world would learn a lot about that mine disaster that saved you from being exposed as a salter. It cost a hundred lives, Grier, but it saved you from prison, didn't it? I know how it happened! I know that gold mine was a fake from start to finish, and I've made sure the world will know if anything happens to me, so bear that in mind—always!"

Grier drew back from him, hands clenched. Darracq was eternally reminding him of the sword that hung over his head. He hated Darracq with a burning hate, but he knew he was helpless to protect himself. Darracq had him cornered like the rat he was, and made no pretence about it.

"I know all that," said Grier. "What is it this time?" He hesitated. "More money? You're getting extravagant, if you don't mind my saying so. Can't you cut it down a bit? My capital won't last long at the rate you go on."

Darracq chuckled. "It'll last long enough," he said. "Besides, I'm on to something now that will make it a whole lot bigger. We're off on safari, Grier, and you'll be paying. I just come along with you, understand? So docs Pierrette, of course."

"This is infamous!" said Grier. But there was little conviction in his tone. It was as if he knew quite well that no matter what objections he raised, Darracq would have his way. Grier was worried about his niece Pierrette, for Darracq had made it quite plain a long time ago that me day he would force the girl to marry him by means of the threat he held over her uncle. Pierrette was devoted to Grier, and would do anything to protect him from the fate that Darracq could call down on his head.

"Cut out the chatter!" snarled Darracq, venomously. "Now listen closely..."

For the next few minutes he talked softly to Grier till the blackmailed man knew as much about the business of Meyrick and Brandon as Darracq did himself.

"We'll do the thing on a grand scale," said Darracq. "There's a young fellow I met a few days ago in town, he's a pilot and has a plane of his own. This is exactly the kind of charter assignment he's looking for. Naturally, he won't be told the full details, but I'll contact him in the morning and fix it up. A light plane will be of immense value in keeping an eye on Meyrick and his outfit."

Grier passed a hand across his face in a gesture of utter weariness. "You're sticking your head out, Darracq," he said. "This thing can only lead to trouble for all of us. Why don't you be satisfied with what you've got, instead of grabbing at something that belongs to someone else?"

Darracq sneered and helped himself to a generous drink from Grier's decanter.

"You're a fool!" he retorted. "When I see something I want to go after it. You're providing the transport this time; I'll provide the brains of the outfit. This is worth a packet to both of us, Grier, so you'd better toe the line, or take the consequences." He thrust his face forward at Grier, mouth slitted dangerously. "You wouldn't want little Pierrette to know all about your gold mine, would you, now? That wouldn't do at all!"

Grier gave up arguing. He had little option, in any event. He knew that until Darracq died there would be no release for himself; yet with Darracq's death would come his own downfall. It was a hopeless situation for a man to be in, but there was nothing Grier could do about it.

White Gold

* * * *

Rex Brandon and his new partner, Meyrick, made their own plans, talking far into the night in Brandon's room at the Hotel Rhodian. It was arranged to leave Bulawayo on the following day. Meyrick had a car in town and Brandon was told that the planter's place was roughly a day's drive away. They would get a few things in town before leaving and stop at one of the kraals en route for the night.

Both men breakfasted early. Brandon left the hotel shortly afterwards to attend to odds and ends of his own business and send off some cables to England. He left Meyrick packing his gear at the hotel.

It was when Brandon was returning about an hour later that his attention was drawn to a big open Packard which had stopped in the middle of the street. A native bullock wagon was pulled across the street, and the driver was engaged in a heated argument with a fair-haired girl who sat behind the wheel of the Packard.

Brandon paused in his stride and stood watching for a moment with a mixture of mild amusement and interest aroused by the girl. She was a very attractive figure, and the flush of impatience that was stealing across her cheeks made here even more so. But she was definitely in trouble of a minor sort.

Brandon walked across the dusty street to the car and stopped alongside the driving seat.

"Anything I can do to sort this out?" he inquired, with a smile.

The girl turned her head, seeing him for the first time.

"That's very kind of you," she said. "I wish you'd make this man understand that I want to get by, and that his wagon is in the way. The bullock's gone lame, or something, according to him."

Brandon nodded. He moved over to the native in charge of the ancient vehicle and addressed him curtly in the local dialect. The driver, seeing that he was now up against a man who would stand no nonsense, hurriedly shifted the wagon. The bullock might be lame, but it wasn't all that bad.

Brandon watched as the cart was moved to make way for the Packard, then he turned and grinned at the girl. She leaned over the side of the car and thanked him.

"Sorry to have been such a nuisance," she murmured, "but I'm not used to dealing with these people and they know it."

Brandon said: "Pleased to have been of assistance."

"Can I drop you anywhere?" she asked.

Brandon hesitated for only a second or two. Then: "If the Hotel Rhodian isn't out of your way I'd be grateful for a lift."

"Jump in," she replied. "I'm passing it, so it'll be no trouble at all."

Brandon sat beside her as she drove through the busy streets. When they reached the Hotel Rhodian he suggested that she had a drink with him. Although it was early she agreed, and the two of them entered the bar.

Meyrick spotted Brandon and wandered across. He shot a sidelong glance at the girl and eyed Brandon inquiringly.

"I'm sorry," said the girl. "My name's Pierrette Grier."

"Mine's Brandon," he said with a grin. "And this is Meyrick. We're partners."

They shook hands all round. Meyrick ordered drinks and the trio chatted amicably for several minutes, after which Pierrette announced her intention of getting back to the hotel where she was staying with her uncle and one of his friends. The men said good-bye, watching as she left them and got into the car again.

It was not until she was gone that Brandon discovered her handbag on the bar stool next to the one on which she had sat while they talked. He ran outside with the bag, but by then the car had disappeared.

Meyrick grinned. "You couldn't have a better excuse for looking her up!" he said. "Go ahead; there's no hurry really as far as we're concerned."

Brandon hid a smile, returned to his unfinished drink and thought about the girl. She had been just the sort he admired. A feminine type, but he thought she'd be capable if things got really tough. The bullock cart episode had not been anything to judge by.

Five minutes later he left the bar with Pierrette's handbag. Meyrick had lent him his car for the short trip to the hotel she had named earlier on. He drove there fast.

Walking in through the entrance foyer, he caught sight of Pierrette in conversation with two men.

To Brandon's amazement he recognised one of them as Darracq, the stranger who had listened in on himself and Meyrick the previous evening. Without faltering in his stride, he advanced on the little group of people. The girl saw him immediately. So did Darracq. Brandon smiled. Darracq muttered something beneath his breath and turned on his heel, disappearing in something of a hurry, obviously annoyed that Brandon should have seen him with the others. It gave Brandon food for thought as the girl stepped forward eagerly to meet him.

A moment later he found himself being introduced to the uncle. Grier was nervous and Brandon was not slow to sense the fact. He stayed with them for only long enough to give Pierrette her handbag and exchange a few pleasantries. Then he returned to the car and drove back to Meyrick, a worried frown on his face.

"I think we ought to look into Grier's activities," said Brandon presently. "It's my belief that the man is up to something; and Darracq's behind it. Where the girl fits in I'm not yet sure."

Meyrick eyed him thoughtfully. "You're making a heap of fuss about it," he chided. "Are you trying to tell me that girl was spying for Darracq? She wasn't that sort!"

"That's what I thought," answered Brandon, doubtfully. "All the same, I don't like it. What about going back to their hotel and nosing round a little? We might pick up another line on Darracq."

Meyrick shrugged. "Just as you like." They left the bar and entered the car, driving off. Brandon left Meyrick in the car round a corner while he himself entered the hotel by a side door. Peering through the bar-lounge entrance, he saw that Grier was talking to a youngish man he knew by sight. The two of them were at a table near a door on the opposite side of the lounge. If Brandon could work his way round without being seen he might listen in to advantage.

It proved an easier manoeuvre than he had anticipated. By the time he arrived at his vantage point, Darracq had joined up with Grier and the other man. Brando remembered that this third member of the party was a charter plane pilot he had met once before. There was certainly nothing crooked about him. His name was Gaynor, Jerry Gaynor. What was he doing with Grier and Darracq? Brandon wondered.

Positioned where he was, Brandon found that he could hear what was being said without much difficulty. There were few people in the lounge at the time. The place was quiet.

Darracq was saying: "What we need, Gaynor, is your plane to act as a recce craft on this elephant hunt we're planning. By using it we can get a good idea of where the beasts are. It will save a great deal of needless trekking because we shall be able to work from a base. Will you charter out the plane and yourself?"

Gaynor considered the question for a moment before making any reply. Then: "Suits me well enough at the usual terms. Let me know when you're leaving and I'll have the kite ready."

3

NEVER TRUST A WOMAN

BRANDON did not wait much longer. He heard a few more of the details and slipped away to re-join Meyrick outside in the car.

"They mean to tag us all right," he said, grimly. "They even intend to use a light aircraft to keep an eye on our movements once we begin. That fellow Darracq is definitely out to get whatever we find."

"What about Grier and the girl?" Brandon shook his head doubtfully. "Grier, I should say at a rough guess, is being dominated or blackmailed into working with Darracq. He obviously doesn't fancy his own position. You've only got to look at him to see how uncomfortable he is!

"As for the girl, I can't believe that she knows what's going on. She didn't strike me as being that type, and in any event she wasn't with Grier and Darracq when they were fixing things up with Gaynor, the pilot."

Meyrick pursed his lips in a sceptical fashion. "I don't trust women much," he grunted. "The entire thing—your chance meeting with Pierrette included—could have been a well-staged bit of play-acting." He looked hard at Brandon. "Do you realise, my friend, that if they could work it so that you became friendly with the girl she might be able to learn a lot of our plans in advance? I don't say you'd give them away, of course, but if she was clever enough she could get to know them without your realising it."

Brandon nodded gloomily. "Yes, I'd thought of that myself," he admitted. "But I still don't believe it; she isn't phoney, I'm positive."

"Maybe she isn't," agreed Meyrick, "but that doesn't mean to say that her uncle and Darracq aren't averse to making use of her without her knowing it!"

"Oh, hell!" exclaimed Brandon. "When can we get out of town and be on our way? The sooner we start the better. Even a short lead on the enemy will be useful, despite Gaynor and his aircraft."

Meyrick grunted and poured himself a drink.

"I suggest we slip out of town at sundown," he said. "We can let it get around that we're staying on here a couple of days, which may, or may not, put Darracq off the scent. They don't know when we're starting, and there's sure to be a certain amount of delay even when they do."

"Very well," murmured Brandon. "That's settled, then! I've done all I want to here, so I'll make it my responsibility to spread false rumours as to when we leave."

Meyrick agreed readily enough. They parted for a time, Brandon going out into the street again, taking the car to be checked at a local garage.

Having left the vehicle in the hands of a mechanic, he started off to walk the few hundred yards to the Hotel Rhodian.

On his way he was nearly killed.

Had it not been for his undoubtedly keen sense of danger, the hit-and-run car would certainly have struck him.

The street he was using at the time was narrow and not over wholesome. Garbage littered it, so that he walked in the centre of its narrow breadth.

It was when he was about half-way down the main road for which he was making that the sound of a car reached his ears. With a vicious snarl of gears, a big saloon shot down the street at a breakneck speed. It was almost broad enough to fill the narrow place, and was rocking from side to side as the driver fought to keep it straight on the uneven beaten earth of the ground.

Brandon had less than a second to realise what was happening. Luckily for him, there was a doorway close at hand. With an instinctive tightening of his muscles he hurled himself from the path of the swiftly approaching car. A native woman was emerging from the doorway as he sprang towards it. They collided on the threshold; then Brandon had forced her backwards with a powerful heave of his mighty shoulders. An instant later the saloon rocketed past.

Brandon, the sweat breaking out on his neck, caught a fleeting glimpse of the driver's face. It was Darracq. Brandon stood where he was for a moment or two. The frightened black woman beside him was staring after the swiftly disappearing car, her mouth wide open. Then she started chattering away in her own language, furious with the driver. Brandon hid a smile as he heard some of the things that Darracq was being called. Not that it worried him much. "He'll get his deserts sooner or later," he told the woman. "It was lucky you didn't step out of that door a moment earlier. You'd have caught it if you had."

Now that the heat of the danger was past she realised what a narrow escape it had been. Her thanks were suddenly profuse. Brandon swept them aside and took his leave of her. He knew there was little sense in proceeding against Darracq for dangerous driving. For one thing, he had not taken a note of the car number, and for another, such a course of action would delay him just as much as it would affect Darracq. It was better, under the circumstances, to ignore the entire thing; but, nevertheless, it was a pointer as to the way things were going to shape. It looked as if it would be war to the death between himself and Darracq.

Brandon smiled in a tight-lipped manner as he strode down the street and made his way back to the Hotel Rhodian.

Neither he nor Meyrick saw anything more of their rivals during the rest of the day. With the coming of darkness they checked out from the hotel and had their luggage carried to the car where it waited at the back door. Bribing the night porter to say nothing of their departure to any inquirers, they took their leave of the place, driving fast out of Bulawayo on the northern road.

Brandon relaxed, letting Meyrick drive. He felt as if he was on the verge of another adventure, and certainly if the curtain raisers were anything to judge by, this one would not be sluggish. Already his fingers were itching to feel the stock of his rifle; to be poised in front of a charging lion or elephant, knowing that his life depended on the accuracy of his aim and the coolness of his nerve.

And behind it all was the knowledge that, combined with the search for the white gold, was the possibility of laying hands on some samples of chromic-ferrous rock formation. If he could work that in as well the time spent on Meyrick's deal would be well worth while.

Driving all night through jungle and plantation land, they arrived at Meyrick's place towards noon next day. Brandon looked round approvingly at the ordered lines of tobacco that stretched for seemingly miles over the well-cultivated ground. Meyrick noticed his interest and was quick to explain how he had bought the plantation in a derelict condition and worked it up to its present state over a period of several years.

Meyrick showed him round with an almost boyish enthusiasm in his own achievements. The whole plantation was entirely self-supporting, having its own pumping station, electricity generating plant and suchlike. The long drying sheds, in which the tobacco leaves were hung in great bunches, were busy, fully a dozen native workers moving around as Meyrick conducted his visitor on a tour of inspection.

The bungalow that Meyrick had built on the foundations of the original one was spacious- and air-conditioned. A cheery and efficient servant was waiting to provide them with a meal and drink on the step when they returned from their stroll round. In the cool of the early evening the two of them discussed their next move.

"I can have a dozen men and two trucks ready to move with all the equipment needed in an hour," said Meyrick. "We can leave whenever you like."

Brandon nodded thoughtfully. He was thinking of the party who would be dogging their steps. The fact that they had left Bulawayo unexpectedly would gain them very little time, for the moment Darracq realised they had gone he only had to find out where Meyrick lived before following. From then it would be a simple matter to take up the trail.

"The further you get with the heavy stuff before they chase us, the better," he said at length. "This is what I suggest. You leave here with the trucks and equipment as soon as you can. Dawn tomorrow, say. I'll stay behind for a day or two, then, if Darracq and Grier arrive, I may be able to stall them off, or find out how much they know. I'll keep the car with me and catch you up when I'm through."

Meyrick considered the suggestion for a while without speaking. Then he nodded agreement and rose to his feet. "I'll give orders to the headman to get cracking," he said. "You won't have any difficulty in following us. I'll leave you Llanga, one of my best Shangaan bearers. He already knows the first part of the route we'll be taking, because he was on safari with me when I found the graveyard. He can lead you easily enough."

Brandon stretched his long legs out in front of him as he reclined in a rhooki chair with a tall glass in one hand and his pipe between his strong white teeth.

"That sounds a very feasible arrangement to me," he commented. "I'm looking forward to a number of various developments in this business. They should all be more or less entertaining." His eyes slitted as he finished.

Meyrick regarded him shrewdly. Then a faint smile touched his mouth, puckering the corners slightly. "The girl..?" he murmured judicially. Brandon shot him an oblique glance and grinned. "Perhaps," he admitted. "But I wasn't thinking of her in particular. The advent of an aircraft on the side of the ungodly intrigues me enormously! There are many possibilities there, you know?" Meyrick said nothing to that.

Shortly afterwards he left the stoep to Brandon and went about the business of getting together his dozen stalwart Shangaan men and assembling the equipment for an early start in the morning. There was little to do, in fact, for everything had been standing at the ready since the day he decided to find a partner in the white gold venture. All that remained to be done was to make final checks on the store trucks.

The sun had barely topped the distant hills to the east when Brandon stood watching the departure next morning.

He raised a hand in salute as the two heavily-laden trucks rumbled out of the compound and disappeared in clouds of dust up the dry hill road leading north.

Then he turned when they were no longer in sight and made his way slowly back to the bungalow.

Llanga, the headman left behind by Meyrick, greeted him with a broad grin. He had already taken a fancy to Brandon and the two of them found much in common, both having had considerable experience on big-game safaris.

The day passed uneventfully, Brandon spending the time in cleaning his rifles and selecting the small amount of camp equipment he meant to take with him when he followed Meyrick.

It was not until noon on the following day, when he was growing restless, that anything happened to quicken his sense of impending adventure.

He had strolled some distance from the bungalow, taking a shot gun with him, and was returning when he heard the sound of a car approaching up the packed dirt road that led to the plantation.

Pausing on a rise of ground that commanded a view of the road, he waited till the vehicle came in sight.

With a silent whistle of interest he saw Pierrette at the wheel of the big Packard roadster. She looked cool and fresh, even in the heat of the blazing noon sun, and the raised hood of the car cast a shadow across her face as she whirled the Packard round a curve and brought it to a rocking halt in the compound fronting the bungalow.

Brandon stood where he was, staring with narrowed eyes as she left the car in the shade of a wide-spreading mopani tree and climbed the broad steps to the veranda of the house.

"Now I wonder what she's up to?" he mused, as he started walking more quickly towards the bungalow.

He saw Llanga meet her at the door of the place. They stood together for a moment, then the girl turned and took seat in one of the rhooki chairs, while Llanga disappeared, presumably to fetch her a drink.

She spotted Brandon when he was still twenty or thirty yards away. He watched as she rose abruptly to her feet, but made no sign himself that he recognised her.

When it was obvious that he could no longer pretend he did not know who she was, he halted, feigning great surprise as she came up to him.

"Why, hello, there!" he said. "What in the world are you doing out here?"

Pierrette smiled warmly. The sun was glinting on her golden hair where it showed beneath the topee she wore.

"I might ask the same of you, Mr. Brandon," she replied gaily. "I certainly never expected to see you when I took this road."

He turned and indicated the bungalow. "Come along in and enjoy what hospitality there is to offer," he said. "If you didn't expect to see anyone you knew, why did you take the road to this plantation?"

She shot him a sidelong glance.

"I was motoring around and lost myself," she answered. "I told you I didn't know the country very well the other day when we met. There was a road fork I mixed up several miles back."

Brandon nodded understandingly. It struck him that she was not making the most of her story. The bungalow was a good day's drive from Bulawayo where she was I supposed to be staying, yet she now said she was driving around. It must have been quite a drive, beginning about midnight. The thought was a sobering one. It could mean only one thing. The girl was lying. She must have known where she was heading for, and she couldn't have started from town. Which led him to believe that her uncle and Darracq were somewhere on the way, probably quite close to Meyrick's plantation.

"Well," he said, cheerfully, "I'm glad you stumbled on me. Sorry I had to leave Bulawayo without saying goodbye, but I had some urgent business that cropped up at the last minute."

She regarded him with wide questioning eyes. He chose to ignore them.

"Are you going on another of your wonderful hunting trips, Mr. Brandon?" she asked when he failed to enlarge.

"Perhaps," he replied. "I can't tell yet. There are lots of things I must do before I can call myself free to do as I please." He laughed. They walked side by side to the veranda steps. At that moment Llanga appeared with a tray of glasses and bottles, setting them down on a small camp table alongside the rhooki chair the girl had recently vacated when she came to meet Brandon.

Brandon leant his shot gun against the wall and drew up a second chair for himself. Pierrette accepted a long, cold glass of iced beer, sipping it as if she really enjoyed it. Brandon wondered vaguely whether she actually did or not.

He said very little himself, forcing the girl to take the initiative. She did not do it very well, and after a few minutes of desultory conversation it became obvious that she was getting nervous and uneasy.

Brandon wished he could help her. He guessed that she had been sent by Darracq or Grier to find out what she could, and a hint of misery that showed in her eyes when he caught her unawares made it plain that she was not enjoying the task. But for all that she was a spy in the camp and he had no intention of coming out into the open till he knew more of the general set-up.

Presently, when Pierrette realised that Brandon would not discuss his plans any more deeply than he had already done, she rose to her feet, thanked him as nicely as she could for his kindness and turned to make her way back to the Packard.

He watched her for a split second, then reached out and touched her arm gently. She turned her head, looking up at him as he stood on the step above her, smiling down in a faintly teasing fashion.

"Have a pleasant ride back to town," he said. "If you start now you ought to get there a little before dawn tomorrow. It's quite a way, you know?"

She caught her lower lip between her teeth for a moment, watching him like a cornered animal, uncertain of what to say or do. Then:

"Thank you," she whispered in a choked voice. "You can say the most extraordinary things when you like, can't you?"

He grinned maliciously. "You do rather odd things, don't you, Pierrette?" he countered. "What are you playing at; that's what I'd like to know."

She bit her lip again, angrily, then turned and almost ran down the steps to the ground.

Brandon called: "Tell Darracq he won't be as lucky as he thinks he is in a while! And tell your uncle from me that he's a fool to be mixed up with Darracq. Goodbye."

The girl never turned her head as she ran for the car.

Brandon watched her. She was ten yards or so from the car when his eyes narrowed suddenly. In a single bound he had whipped across the veranda and grabbed up his gun. An instant later he dropped on one knee, cuddling the stock to his cheek. Pierrette was close to the Packard now.

4

WORDS OF FOREBODING

PIERRETTE saw the venomous snake ait the same moment as Brandon fired. She bit back a cry of alarm, recognising a mamba, most poisonous and dangerous reptile in the world. Then Brandon's shot shattered the head of the creature and splashed its blood on the side of the car as it reared up within inches of the girl, to fall back dead.

The girl shrank away, staring at the dead snake in a kind of fascinated horror, as she realised the narrowness of her escape. Another step or two and she would have trodden on it. If Brandon hadn't— She turned her head, wrenching herself from the thought, to meet the man who had saved her life.

Brandon strode towards her, the smoking shot gun still grasped in his hand. The muscles of his face were taut as he met her gaze,

"It must have dropped from the mopani tree," he said. "Are you all right? Sorry I had to shoot so close to you, Pierrette, but it was tricky. Shot gun wasn't an ideal weapon, either, with you so near to target." He grinned at her forgivingly, then gestured wryly to the pellet-spattered running-board of the Packard. "Your uncle won't thank me for doing that," he added.

Pierrette swallowed painfully. She was not in an easy position, and knew it. With an effort she found her tongue, silently thanking Brandon for talking as fast as he could and saving her the trouble till she'd collected her wits.

"You—you saved my life," she stammered blankly. "How can I say anything? I'm not hurt—physically. But I—"

Brandon grinned and cut her short. "Shook you, didn't it?" he murmured. "Come and have another drink. Steady your nerve before driving back to Bulawayo." He could not resist the last jibe, in spite of himself. It was mean to take advantage of her like that, he thought, a little bitterly.

She gulped in her throat and stared back at him. Then: "Oh, what's the use?" she said in a whisper. "I'm no good at this game! All I've done is make a mess of it." Brandon said nothing, but cocked an eyebrow at her. Then he took her firmly by the arm and led her back to the stoep. Llanga had rushed from inside the bungalow at the sound of the shot. Brandon caught his eye.

"There's a dead mamba by the car," he said. "Shift it, will you?"

Llanga nodded violently. "I'll do it; you leave him to me!"

The girl sank into a chair and tried to get a hold on herself while Brandon poured her a brandy and soda.

"Drink that," he said, almost curtly.

She took the glass without protest, then set it down again without tasting it.

"I've behaved like a heel," she announced. "I came here to spy on you; to find out what your plans were; how far you'd go in this hunt for ivory. And in return you save my life." She stared at him morosely. "What kind of person do you imagine that makes me feel?"

Brandon regarded her unsmilingly for a moment.

"You didn't fool me," he said. "It was all so patently obvious that I wasn't taken in for an instant. I should have expected better of you, but I've no hard feelings. Why did you do it?"

She dropped her gaze. "It wasn't from choice," she said. "Please believe that! I had to do it, don't you understand?"

Brandon nodded. "Go on," he said. "Darracq, I take it? He's got something on your uncle, hasn't he?"

She gave a deep sigh. "Yes," she admitted. "I'm so ashamed, and it makes it worse, because I don't even know what uncle did to put himself in this man's clutches. In fact, I didn't know a thing about it until yesterday, when I happened to overhear them talking. Then I guessed a lot of things. Darracq made me come on this safari with them. He said uncle would suffer prison if I didn't do as he said."

"It's a dirty game," muttered Brandon. "You can help to cancel it out by telling me all you know. Will you do that before you leave here?"

She thought for a moment. Her face was drawn and not in the least happy. "All right," she said at length. "As I understand it, you and Mr. Meyrick are after some ivory, or something of the sort. Darracq wants to get it for himself, and is using uncle as a means to an end. The general idea is to let you and Meyrick find the stuff, while Darracq and our party follows. When you've got it they'll take it off you."

Brandon thrust his hands into the pockets of his duck trousers, grinning boyishly as he watched her.

"That's exactly what I figured out for myself," he said. "Now, finish your drink and get back to uncle. You don't have to say you've failed; or mention what happened hi detail. Tell Darracq that you found out Meyrick has already gone on ahead and that I'm following him in the morning. Say you weren't able to find out the route I'd follow, but that it leads more .or less north from here. You needn't say any more than that. Darracq should be satisfied."

Pierrette stared at him gratefully. "You've been wonderful!" she said. "Thank you a hundred times—for saving my life, as well as taking what I've done the way you have."

Brandon smiled down at her. "We shall meet again, I hope." He paused, holding out his hand. Then, as she gripped it: "If you're badly in trouble at any time don't hesitate to turn this way."

"Thank you," she whispered. "You make me feel very small. Next time we meet I hope it will be on a different footing. Now, I'd better go."

"Good luck," said Brandon, quietly. This time he walked right to the car with her and closed the door when she was seated behind the wheel. She drove out of the compound fast, not looking back at him as he stood and watched her go.

With tightened lips he turned on his heel and ran back to the bungalow. Llanga was standing in the open doorway, waiting for him.

"Is the car loaded, Llanga?" demanded Brandon. "We're moving at once. That was one of our rivals! She isn't bad, but they're using her—either as a spy or as bait!"

Llanga looked at him goggle-eyed for an instant.

"The bwana means it?" he said. He shook his head as if he did not understand the ways of white men. Then he and Brandon were making for the loaded car where it stood out of sight in the rear of the bungalow. The headman of the plantation staff saw them off. He already had his orders, and would carry them out to the letter. Meyrick had picked his men well when he staffed the plantation.

Brandon started the car, a big, cool-running saloon. The engine sounded odd as he revved it up, listening. Not until then did he realise there was another noise beating on the rhythm of the motor.

Llanga looked at him curiously, wondering what the matter was. Brandon switched off the engine again and sat very still .in his seat.

Clearly to their ears came the steady drone of a light aircraft motor.

Brandon turned his head and grinned at Llanga.

"The mulungu are keeping an eye on us," he murmured.

"Inkosi," said Llanga, "are these mulungu very bad? We could wait and kill them before we start."

"Sounds a simple thing the way you put it," answered Brandon with a laugh. "It isn't quite as easy as that, I'm afraid! No, we'll lie up where we are for a few minutes till that plane has finished looking round." Llanga nodded. He was clearly disappointed, but his respect for Brandon was enormous. Whatever the tall hunter said was law as far as he was concerned.

They sat in the car, listening to the rising note of the aircraft. It increased in volume till it sounded as if it was almost overhead, circling. Brandon caught a glimpse of it as it dipped out of sight below a copse of big mopani trees. He wondered who was piloting it; whether Darracq was passenger. He guessed that the plane had come this way with the object of seeing if Pierrette was still at the bungalow. Or, more probably, whether a safari party was in view, or on the point of leaving the plantation.

Ten minutes later there was no sound of the aircraft's engine. It had turned and faded out as it winged its way south again.

"Right!" said Brandon. "Now we can get on our way, Llanga."

"Yes, Inkosi."

Brandon pressed the starter button again and the motor hummed into life. Soon they were clear of the plantation and striking along a rutted dirt road that was hemmed in on both sides by densely-growing scrub-thorn and baobab trees. Brandon drove swiftly, for he wanted to make as much time as he could after the delay at the bungalow. His thoughts were mixed, as the road began to climb through tangled groves of jungle. On several occasions he glimpsed small game as it scampered across the road in front of the car.

"We shall arrive at Mahambe's kraal by night-fall," said Llanga solemnly. "That is good, for there is always news to be learnt round the fires."

Brandon shot him a glance. "What sort of news?" he inquired.

"Of elephants, Inkosi. There are rumours already."

"The more the merrier," said Brandon. "But you know what Mr. Meyrick is after, don't you?"

Llanga nodded without speaking. "There will be much trouble, bwana, that I feel in my bones."

Brandon silently agreed, but he did not think the trouble would come from disturbing the sanctity of an elephants' graveyard for the sake of white gold. It was far more likely to come from Darracq and the outfit he led. Poor Pierrette, he thought. She was certainly a child of grim circumstance.

Pressing on fast up hill and down dale, through dense scrub and tall growing tracts of forest, Brandon and Llanga kept thrusting north, towards the Matan Hills. Somewhere ahead of them was Meyrick, but his pace would be considerably less than theirs, for the heavy trucks were slow in comparison with the car.

Dusk was falling by the time Llanga intimated that they were nearing Mahambe's kraal.

Before long Brandon swept the car off the dusty road and took it up a narrow track, which ended in a Shangaan village. There the two of them were greeted by the headman, a wizen old fellow with mud-plastered hair and heavily tattooed face. In spite of his fearsome appearance, Slovu proved a genial host, and Brandon was glad they had stopped instead of pressing on.

Sitting round the headman's hut fire that night there was much talk, mostly on the subject of hunting.

"Inkosi," said Slovu presently, "your man tells me you are a great white hunter. There is something in the district which will interest you."

"Tell it, induna," answered Brandon, solemnly.

"A large herd of elephants is reported to be moving up the opposite bank of the Schissra River, further north," said the headman quietly. "When your friends with the lorries went by yesterday I told them the same, but the bwana said he might not be able to hunt them, for he is keeping to the west bank."

"That is of great interest, Slovu," replied Brandon with a grave smile. "I can move more quickly than my friend. Perhaps I shall be able to get a shot at one of the elephants. If I do, it will be thanks to you."

The headman smiled and nodded. "It is my pleasure to be of help to the white man," he replied. "Now you and your man must sleep, for you will wish to leave early."

Llanga had already pitched Brandon's tent on the edge of the village, and with solemn good-nights the little party broke up.

On the move again at dawn, Brandon wasted no time in making what speed he could, though the going was getting more and more uneven as the road, which was little used, gradually deteriorated. In parts it was grown right over with thorn. Brandon sent the car charging at it, breaking through with the sound of cracking wood and torn foliage. Halting at noon, they refilled the tank from jerry cans carried in the car. Llanga prepared a hasty meal; then they were off .again.

The shadows were lengthening with coming dusk when Llanga pointed ahead to a drift of smoke where it rose behind a thick clump of baobob trees. "Inkosi Meyrick," he announced. Brandon gave a nod and presently the car was brought to a stop in a clearing just off the road. The two heavy trucks were backed into the clearing. Meyrick's 'boys' were making camp, while Meyrick himself bustled round supervising the operation, a rifle under his arm and a big revolver strapped to his rotund waist. He wore shorts and puttees, a crumpled bush shirt and sun helmet, which was now tipped to the back of his bald head.

At sight of Brandon and Llanga, he hurried forward, a broad grin on his perspiring face.

"Hello, there!" he called. "You made better time than I dared to hope! Anything happened? What about Grier and that devil Darracq? Are they on our tails?"

Brandon stepped from the car and stretched his arms. He was stiff and not sorry to walk about instead of riding. "One question at a time!" he grinned. "There's nothing to worry about at the moment. We're well ahead of them at present, but they're using that plane for recce. I saw it just before leaving the plantation."

Meyrick nodded grimly. "We'll give 'em a run for their money!" he said, with conviction.

Brandon walked beside him towards Meyrick's tent. Llanga was unpacking the camp gear from the car, while the other Shangaans clustered round him, asking questions and exchanging news.

Brandon said: "They sent the girl out to see if they could learn anything from me. It didn't work out from her point of view; in the end she lost her nerve and told me a few things!"

He did not mention having saved her life from the mamba.

Later on, when they were sitting down to a meal outside Meyrick's tent, Brandon passed on the information about the large herd of elephants reported in the district.

Meyrick grunted. "We strike the river fairly soon," he said. "Our path lies on the western bank, but if the herd is moving up the east side you might as well have a crack at 'em on your own. Take Llanga with you."

"Thanks." Brandon decided to try his luck. "We ought to strike the river about noon to-morrow," he murmured.

Again Meyrick nodded. "Not far out," he said.

The night was quiet, apart from the constant chatter of monkeys and the rustle of small nocturnal creatures in the thick undergrowth round the camp site. Brandon slept in a state of undisturbed relaxation. He was tired from the previous day's drive, and although his mind was full of all that had happened, he was so well disciplined in himself that years before he had learnt the knack of shutting out thoughts and sleeping as and when he desired.

While the bearers were packing the trucks and gear on the following morning, Brandon and Meyrick went ahead on a short reconnaissance in the car. The road had almost vanished by this time, and from now on they would be penetrating bush country of an even wilder nature than before. Picking a route for the heavy trucks was a tricky business, but in the end they had mapped out the line of advance for several miles ahead. Then they returned to the camp, to find that Llanga and the other Shangaan headman were already moving off in their wake, bringing the trucks.

By mid-day they were halted once more on the low-lying bank of a broad, shallow river. Brilliantly coloured flamingos flocked on the farther shore, taking off every now and then in a vast pink cloud as the sun caught their plumage. They would fly round in a wide circle, then settle again in almost the same place as before. Smaller birds mingled with them. Even from that distance their shrill cries were audible to the white men across the stretch of water.

Brandon stood for a time in silent contemplation, as he stared across the river. Meyrick came up beside him, a faint smile on his lips, as he guessed what his partner was thinking.

"You're pretty keen to go after those elephants, aren't you?" he murmured, mopping his brow as he spoke. "Well, if you want to, Rex, you're welcome! Personally, I can't think of anything more exhausting, but that's your affair!"

Brandon grinned. "I'll keep Llanga back and catch you up later on," he said. "If we don't find any spoor of the herd by night-fall, I promise to carry on and follow you."

"Fair enough!" agreed Meyrick. "Leave the car this side of the river. You'll be using your own feet this time."

Brandon called for Llanga.

"The Inkosi wishes something?" he inquired, with a broad grin.

"Yebbo," Brandon answered. "You and I are after those elephants, Llanga. Bring enough food for one day. I'll get the rifles. We leave at once."

"Yessir!" replied Llanga with alacrity. He darted off at the double, while Brandon strolled back to the car, where he picked up his heavy-bore elephant gun and checked it carefully. He selected a smaller-bore weapon in case they ran up against lighter game than expected.

Half an hour later the two of them were off. Llanga carried the stores on his head. Brandon brought the two rifles and ammunition. Together they waded into the water, crossing the broad but shallow flow without difficulty. A few crocodiles showed interest in them during the crossing, but one shot by Brandon was sufficient to deter them from coming any closer. Llanga, making a tremendous splashing as he waded along, added to the disturbance, so that they were not attacked.

On the far bank they rested for a minute or two, waving to Meyrick, who stood watching them from the distant shore.

"Now then," said Brandon. "Come on, Llanga; there's work to do. I'd be as pleased as anything if we could take a decent pair of tusks back to camp when we cross again!"

Llanga grinned. "We shall see, bwana," he said. "It would be good, I agree, but men can never foresee the things that will happen when they plan the future for themselves."

Brandon eyed him curiously for an instant. Had he been a superstitious man he might have taken Llanga's words more seriously. Even as it was, they sent a faint chill through his flesh in spite of his iron-hard nerves. Little did he know what the future would hold.

"Yes," he mused, slowly. "We shall see, Llanga. Come on now!"

5

THE DESOLATION

DUMPING most of their kit, Brandon and his black companion made a wide cast round the spot at which they had crossed the river. At first Brandon thought they were out of luck, but when his spirits were beginning to sink a muttered exclamation from Llanga brought him running up beside him. Llanga was kneeling on the ground, his face close to the damp earth.

"Much spoor, Inkosi," he whispered. "It is not very old, either!" There was a note of excitement in his voice.

Brandon saw at a glance that the man was right. Llanga was examining the track of one great animal, but, by looking a little further afield, they came on the spoor of fully a score of the beasts.

"They must have passed in the night," said Brandon. "By the look of it they're only a few hours in front of us."

"We follow, bwana?"

Brandon nodded firmly. "You bet we do!" he returned.

Hurrying back to the spot at which they had left the gear, they started off on the trail of the slowing-moving herd. It was plain that the elephants were feeding as they went, not hurriedly as they would do if pursued, but with a finnicky choice of leaves and wild fruits from the trees they passed.

Pushing on through the steamy heat of the thorn scrub vegetation, Brandon and Llanga took up the chase.

They trekked as swiftly as the going permitted, always following the line of advance left by the elephant herd.

Evening was coming down. Brandon thought they would have to give up the chase till morning, but Llanga told him the spoor was so fresh now that the beasts could not be more than a mile or so ahead.

Brandon decided to push on, in spite of the growing dusk.

A clearing opened in front of them. Llanga paused on the edge of it, peering through the semi-darkness, head on one side, as he listened for the slightest sound.

Brandon, tense at his side, his heavy-bore rifle gripped firmly in his hands, waited breathlessly.

Suddenly, from the monstrous shadow of a clump of dense mchwili trees on the far side of the clearing, they heard a rumbling grunt and a flapping sound. An instant later the mighty bulk of a great bull elephant broke cover and came towards them at a fast run, trunk raised, ears spread wide.

Llanga uttered a gasp. Brandon dropped to one knee and brought his rifle up at the same time. The big bull came on till it was no more than fifteen yards from him, bellowing angrily as it thundered over the ground.

Brandon held his fire till the last possible moment. He felt, rather than saw, Llanga dart away, for cover. Then his rifle crashed in the air and the bull elephant seemed to check in the middle of a stride. It was an incredible sight, for it was just as if the great beast had met an invisible wall.

With a groan it sank to its knees as Brandon dispatched it with a second well-placed bullet. When it rolled on its side it was less than eight or nine yards from him.

He stood up, conscious of a flush of triumph coursing through his veins as Llanga reappeared from the cover of the bush.

"We were lucky, Llanga," he said, quietly. "Now we have a pair of tusks worth having!"

They set to and hacked out the pair of enormous tusks from the elephant's skull.

"If we hurry we can make the river again and cross in the morning," said Brandon. "I shouldn't risk a crossing in darkness."

"The Inkosi is wise," answered Llanga with a sagacious nod of his head. "I will carry the ivory."

With one tusk balanced on each shoulder, he set off at a brisk pace, leading Brandon back by the way they had come. A full moon, rising shortly after dark, lit their path, but, even so, it was well after midnight by the time they arrived at the spot where they had crossed the river. Had it not been for the fact that they had left the car opposite, Brandon would have crossed higher upstream, but, as it was, he was forced to back-track in this way.

They camped on the river bank, lighting a fire and cooking a meal. There was no sign of life from the direction of the opposite shore. Brandon knew that Meyrick had intended to move on as soon as he himself split away with Llanga. By now he and the main party would be many miles up-country, much closer to the fabulous white gold horde that was their aim.

With the first hint of dawn the two men packed their gear and waded into the shallow river. Burdened with the extra weight of the tusks, the crossing took longer than before, but at last Brandon felt the yielding mud of the actual bank beneath his feet. Splashing through the thin reeds that-.grew at the water's edge, he scrambled on to dry land and stood waiting for Llanga.

The site of Meyrick's old camp was hidden by trees from where they were. Brandon started off through the scrub, whistling softly to himself as he strode along. Then he came to a sudden halt. Llanga almost bumped into his back. Brandon gripped his rifle more tightly and levered a cartridge into the breech, eyes darting from side to side as he sought some clue to the scene of desolation before him.

"Bwana, what has happened?" gasped Llanga, breathlessly.

"I don't know; but I mean to find out, Llanga!" muttered Brandon grimly. He started forward more slowly, rifle thrust out in front of him.

The car stood where he had left it, on the edge of the camp he and Meyrick had made. Brandon had expected it to be alone, but this was not the case. The two heavy trucks were still parked where they had been before.

But it was not so much that fact which troubled Brandon as the sight of several of Meyrick's Shangaans lying on the ground with spears thrust into their glistening bodies and the blood dry and black on their skins.

"Natives have done this," muttered Brandon. "But why should they, Llanga? And where is Meyrick?"

He and the black quickly started searching through the little camp for signs of Meyrick and the other 'boys'. It was Brandon who found his partner.

Meyrick lay stretched on the ground behind a fallen tree, a shot gun grasped in his fingers and an ugly-looking bruise above his right eye. It took little time for Brandon to discover, with a sigh of relief that his partner was not only breathing, but just on the point of coming round.

Reaching for his flask, Brandon forced some of the fiery spirit down Meyrick's throat, sitting back on his heels to watch for results. They came quickly. Meyrick struggled up on one elbow, shook his head and grabbed his gun, glaring at Brandon as if he did not at first recognise him.

"Hey, take it easy," said Brandon. "It's me, not the enemy! What happened, man?"

Meyrick took another drink from the flask, rubbed a hand over his face and grimaced with pain as he touched his head.

"Some tribe of natives attacked us," he grunted.

"When?"

"Last evening."

Brandon frowned. "But I thought you were going on as fast as you could?" he said in a puzzled tone.

"So I was, but one of the trucks was giving a bit of trouble, so we stayed over till it was put right. The men were getting the evening meal when they attacked us."

"What happened to you?"

"Throwing club got me! I came to in the night, but felt so weak and sick I just collapsed again. Guess I've been asleep ever since."

It was at this juncture that Llanga came up and stood by. Brandon glanced up at him inquiringly.

"Bwana, I have found one of the fatherless sons of darkness who did this thing," he announced. "He is yonder, but is wounded."

Brandon nodded. "Thanks," he said. "I'll go and see him. How many of the party are missing?"

"Bwana," said Llanga sadly, "I have discovered seven dead, but the rest must have run away. They will return soon, for the sun is up and will give them courage."

"Take me to this wounded enemy!" Llanga gave one look at Brandon's angry features and led the way without a word. The wounded man had been shot in both legs, and was obviously in great pain. Brandon took a look at his wounds and dispatched Llanga to get the first-aid kit. While he was gone he eyed the man sternly.

"From what tribe do you come?" he demanded.

The man stared back at him sullenly. "If I tell you the white man's law will strike my kraal!" he retorted.

"Perhaps not—if you tell me what I ask."

"I shall die of my wounds," said the man. Brandon shook his head. "They aren't serious. If you do not talk and tell me what I want to know, you will die in the hands of the white man's hangman! Think on that!'

"I am a Durlenk, Inkosi," said the man after a moment's pause. "It was not my people who put this thing in our heads, but another mulungu with a clever tongue."

Brandon gave a nod. "Go on," he said sternly. "What did he tell you?"

"That you and your friend and Shangaans were coming here to kill and plunder our stock and our game. That you were thieves and murderers escaping from the law you enforced."

"So you came and attacked the camp, eh? Where is the mulungu who told you these false things?"

"He and his friends are not far away. They have great flying-machine and many men with them. They are after you."

Brandon stood up and watched him thoughtfully for a second or two in silence. Then: "I will tend your wounds man of Durlenk," he said. "They will mend and you will hunt again, but you will return to your tribe and tell them that punishment will come to the kraal if they listen to the false tongues of strangers and bad mulungus."

The man gave a nod. His eyes were wide, partly from surprise and partly from relief. "Yebbo, Inkosil" h said. "It shall be as you say."

Llanga returned with the first-aid case. He was followed a moment afterwards by Meyrick, swaying a little as he walked, but nevertheless on his feet again.

Brandon dressed the Durlenk's wounded legs. They had taken a charge of shot-gun pellets in the calves and would be painful for a long time. While he worked he talked to Meyrick:

"Darracq brought this on us," he said. "He told the natives we were a bad lot and set them stirring up trouble. I'm going back down the trail to locate Darracq's parry and do a bit of spying myself. It's going a little too far when they turn the natives against us and kill our men,"

Meyrick pursed his lips. "Watch you step," he warned.

"Don't worry," answered Brandon. "Darracq tried to wipe me out once back in Bulawayo; he won't be fool enough to show his hand so plainly next time. Besides, I know what to expect from him now." He broke off. "The only thing that puzzles me a little is what he hoped to gain by getting the Durlenks to attack the camp. Did he think you'd be killed? If that happened he'd lose all chance of finding the graveyard by trailing us."

Meyrick considered the problem. At length: "I don't think they intended to have us killed," he said. "If they had done, why was I left alive? They could have finished me off with the greatest of ease once they knocked me cold." He paused, thinking things out. Then: "If you ask me, this attack was a sort of harrying operation. Darracq wanted to delay and hinder us, reduce the odds perhaps, but he didn't want to stop us. If you'd been here at the time you might have been killed, which would have suited him all right, but he guessed that it wouldn't have stopped me carrying on."

Brandon nodded. "Probably the Durlenk chief was told to do what he could without killing the white men in the party. That would fit the case well enough."

He glanced round. Llanga was standing by, watching closely, taking in all that was said. The wounded Durlenk warrior scowled from his position on the ground.

"Keep this man with you till he can walk," advised Brandon slowly. "I shan't be any longer than I can help."

Meyrick nodded thoughtfully. "Fine!" he said with a rueful grin. He looked up at a noise from the edge of the clearing where the camp was situated. A moment later two of the missing Shangaan bearers appeared. They came towards Meyrick with a guilty air. Three more followed them at a distance.

"Here's your men back with their tails between their legs," grunted Brandon. "I'll be seeing you."

"Are you taking Llanga with you?"

"Not this time. What I am to do is work on my own for a change."

"The Commando touch, eh?" Meyrick laughed softly.

Brandon selected one of his high-velocity medium-bore rifles with a fifteen shot magazine and loaded it to capacity. "Leave the car where it is," he said to Meyrick. "I'll pick it up from here when I get back. You push on as fast as you can. Put the men to burying the dead. I shall probably re-join you tonight."

Meyrick agreed to the plan. Brandon set off a few minutes afterwards when he had questioned the Durlenk and discovered more exactly the whereabouts of Darracq and Grier.

Little did he know as he struck off through the scrub what developments the next few hours would bring.

6

THE FUGITIVE

ACCORDING to the information obtained from the wounded warrior, Grier and Darracq were no more than half a day's trek to the south. Brandon moved swiftly down the barely defined trail, pausing every now and again to listen. Once he thought he heard the drone of the aircraft in the distance, but it did not show itself overhead. Probably Darracq was keeping it for more important missions at a later date. He wondered whether Jerry Gaynor, the pilot, realised what was going on. The odds were that he did not, for he was not the type of man to countenance anything of an evil nature.

Thrusting his way through dense, tangled thorn scrub and thickets of baobob trees, Rex Brandon covered the ground with the skill of a man with years of jungle experience behind him. The heat was not yet overpowering, and the foliage above his head offered shelter. Birds and monkeys made raucous music in the branches above. Once he froze in his tracks as his keen eyes glimpsed a yellow and black spotted shape slinking through the undergrowth forty or fifty yards away. It was not in his plan to shoot a leopard, and he waited a while till the beast disappeared. With the enemy but a short distance ahead of him, Brandon wanted to avoid shooting if he possibly could. The crack of a rifle would carry a considerable way in the jungle that hemmed him in on all sides.

Noon found Brandon on the banks of a stream that fed into the big river east of where he was. He halted for a brief rest, drinking water from his canteen and eating some of the ready-prepared food that Llanga had packed before he left camp.

It was while he was making up his mind as to what line to take when he located Darracq's safari that a half-stifled cry reached his ears.

Instantly on the alert, he seized his rifle and sprang to his feet, listening intently.

The cry was repeated, closer now. It held a note of terror that galvanised Brandon into movement. Even as he started running in the direction from which the cry had come the jungle reverberated with the deep-throated growling roar of a lion.

Crashing through the undergrowth, heedless of the thorns that tore at his clothes, Brandon broke out into a clearing. Staring round anxiously, he beheld a scene that brought him to an abrupt halt.

In the middle of the clearing was a tall mopani tree. There was a profusion of scrub at its base, which was now in a state of agitation as some violently-moving body leapt through the tangle. Clinging to the lowest branch of the mopani tree, her feet only a short distance from the top of the scrub, was Pierrette.

Even as Brandon took in the scene the tawny shape of a thickly-maned killer lion sprang upwards, narrowly missing the girl's legs as she swung them out of reach with an effort.

"Hang on!" yelled Brandon. He brought up his rifle and sighted as the lion whirled round, sensing fresh danger.

The sharp crack of the rifle and the bellowing roar of the animal were simultaneous. Then it rolled over and over in the scrub, threshing and tearing at the foliage in its dying agony.

Brandon ran across the clearing. The lion found some new reserve of energy, struggling to its feet again. At the same instant Pierrette's grip on the mopani tree broke and she dropped like a stone, landing within a foot or two of the lion.

Brandon halted, fired again as the lion leapt at the girl. The bullet knocked the beast sideways. Then Brandon had a grasp on her shoulder and was wrenching her out of harm's way.

But the lion was finished. Brandon's second bullet had taken it clean in the heart, and now it lay dead at their feet.

Pierrette shuddered violently as her eyes met those of Brandon.

Instinctively his arm went round her shoulders, steadying her shaking body.

"It's all right," he said reassuringly. While he was speaking a dozen questions were running through his mind. His eyes raked the undergrowth, expecting at any moment to see Darracq break into view.

But nothing happened.

"You...you seem to make a habit of saving, my life," the girl stammered nervously. "I honestly don't know what to say."

"Forget it!" he answered curtly. "What are you doing out here in the bush? Where are the rest of your party?"

Pierrette swallowed uneasily. "They—they're after me," she muttered.

"After you! What do you mean?" Brandon frowned.

"I couldn't stand it any longer," she replied. "I ran away early this morning, trying to catch up with you. They mean to kill you all as soon as it suits them. Darracq was fixing something up with some natives yesterday." Her eyes were wide with anxiety.

Brandon grunted. He was somewhat annoyed with the girl, for in one way she was presenting a problem.

"If you're running away," he said slowly, "I suppose that means you can't return?"

She shook her head firmly. "No," she said. "I was hoping I'd catch up with you, but if you don't want me in your safari I'll turn round and trek back to civilisation."

Brandon laughed gently. "You wouldn't find it all that simple," he answered. "Is Darracq close on your tail?"

"I can't tell," she answered. "I slipped away at dawn, but it wouldn't have taken them long to find out I was gone. Darracq has some fine trackers in the party."

"So I imagine… We'd better be moving, Pierrette. If you can't return to your own camp you'll have to join us. There's no middle way in the jungle!"

The girl looked at him for a moment in silence. Then: "You won't regret taking me on," she replied. "I promise not to be a nuisance."

Brandon hid a smile. "Time will tell," he said.

Pierrette dropped her gaze. "I am a nuisance, aren't I?" she said. "I know it; but what else could I do?"

"Nothing," he replied hurriedly. "Forgive me if I sound a little put out about it. I wasn't expecting to take on the added responsibility of a woman on this trip." The girl opened her mouth to speak, then turned her head in a startled fashion at the sound on the other side of the big mopani tree.

Brandon, too, whirled round. Watching them where they stood close to the carcase of the dead lion, was Darracq. A thin smile creased his face, but there was no friendship, or humour in the expression. He balanced a revolver in one hand as he advanced on them cautiously. "Don't try the brave man act!" he warned harshly. Brandon stood perfectly still, assessing the chances as Darracq approached. He realised that the man had probably been listening in to most of what they had said. Now it seemed that a showdown would be forced between them.

Darracq glanced at Pierrette shrewdly. "Running out on your poor old uncle, eh?" he sneered. "You're a fine person! Going over to the enemy, too! I might have known what to expect, but I thought you'd be pleasant company on the journey."

Brandon watched as the man came closer. He cursed himself for having leant his rifle against the tree. Now he was unarmed and Darracq could shoot him down if he chose to. Not that he thought he would in front of the girl. The risk would be too great afterwards, unless he killed her as well. Brandon had a strong suspicion that Darracq felt too much about her to do a thing like that, in spite of his taunting, sneering tone of address.

The man reached out with his free hand and gripped the girl's wrist. For an instant the revolver wavered from its aim on Brandon's stomach. Brandon tensed himself and lunged out sideways. Throwing himself out and down he got a grip on the revolver and wrenched it round just as Darracq swore and fired wildly. The heavy bullet ploughed into the ground at Brandon's feet. Pierrette screamed and tore herself free of Darracq. Then Brandon's balled-up fist whipped up and smashed like a pile-driver into the man's face. With a grunt he collapsed, sagging at the knees, as Brandon drove another blow to the point of his chin.

With Darracq a crumpled heap on the ground, he turned and looked at Pierrette, who had picked up the man's revolver and was aiming it at Darracq.

"Well," he said, quietly, rubbing his knuckles gently, "we seem to have dealt with him in a satisfactory manner! But what the devil are we going to do with the man?"

"I don't know," she said. Her voice was nervous. "Strictly speaking, we ought to take him with us, keep him a prisoner and hand him over to the police when we get back off the trek. But I don't want that if it can be helped.

"Couldn't you leave him here?" she suggested. "Take his gun and ammunition and just leave him. He'll find his way back."

Brandon grinned, looking from the girl to Darracq, who was breathing noisily through his open mouth.

"You're not particularly malicious towards him," he said.

"It isn't that exactly. But if you don't want him as a prisoner there's nothing else you can do, is there?" Her tone was reasonable now; all the fear seemed to have left her.

Brandon nodded. "All right, then," he said. "Just as you say. You've got his gun, so stick to it." He bent down and unlaced Darracq's boots and took them off, then emptied his pockets of everything he could find. There was nothing of value or importance brought to light by the search.

Brandon stood upright. "Come on," he said firmly. "If we hang around any longer we shall have half their bearers chasing us. I've no quarrel with them!"

The girl eyed him approvingly.

Brandon took a piece of paper from his pocket and wrote something on it in pencil, then pinned the sheet to Darracq's bush-shirt.

Pierrette leant over and read what he had written.

"You were lucky that time, Darracq," she read aloud. "Next time we meet I shan't be so gentle. Take my advice and get back to wherever you belong before something happens to you. Rex Brandon." She paused. "Sounds good!" she added reflectively. "Rex Brandon, I mean."

"Come on!" he said a little impatiently. "We've a long way to go before evening."

With a final glance round, they set off. Brandon forced the pace as much as he dared, and was thankful to find that Pierrette had little difficulty in keeping up with him. Neither of them said very much on the way, for the going was rough. Brandon, who would have liked to ask a number of questions, held his tongue till there was an opportunity of talking in comfort.

Pierrette, on her part, said little of the things that were going on in her mind. She was a prey to anxiety regarding her uncle, but the discoveries she had recently made about his nefarious past had done a lot to damage her faith in him, which, hi turn, had undermined her affection towards him.

They halted for a short rest about half-way back to the place where Brandon had left the car. During the several minutes they sat in the shade of a wide-spreading mchwili tree Pierrette gave him details of the last few days.

"What about Gaynor's aeroplane?" Brandon asked when she had finished. "It hasn't been in evidence much since the time you came to Meyrick's bungalow."

She shook her head. "They haven't been able to use it as much as they expected," she told him. "It can only land in big clearings, of course, and then they have to leave it behind with Gaynor till they find another suitable place further on."

"Tell me," he said quietly, as he leaned back and smoked his pipe, "where does Jerry Gaynor figure in the set-up? He isn't aware of what's really happening, is he?"

Again the girl shook her head. "He's nice," she said. "But the first day out he sprained a wrist and hasn't been doing much flying since. Darracq handles the plane when it goes up. I don't think Jerry knows what it's all about."

"Pity you couldn't have brought him along with you when you walked out on them," said Brandon regretfully. "I knew Jerry slightly. He's a good sort, but if they think he's getting inquisitive they'll take steps to silence him—for always, if he isn't careful."

"That's just what I'm afraid of myself," said Pierrette slowly. "Isn't there something we can do?"

"Later on, maybe; not now. My one aim is to catch up with Meyrick as quickly as possible. The scrub's getting pretty dense further on, so we shan't be able to use the trucks or the car much longer. We've got to cover as much ground as we can. After that, it'll be a question of trekking on foot."

"Where are you going, exactly?" she queried.

Brandon shot her a glance of mingled amusement and the hint of doubt. "I can't tell you," he replied. "Even if you were trying to find out for other reasons than plain curiosity I shouldn't tell you, because I don't know for sure."

She flushed. "I was only curious," she answered.

Brandon grinned a little. "Don't let's quarrel," he said gravely. "Better things to do. Time we were on our way again."

The girl scrambled to her feet as he picked up his rifle and water bottle. Then they were plodding on once more through the thickening undergrowth, following the trail left by Meyrick's trucks earlier on.

The sun was sinking by the time Brandon sighted the car and gave a sigh of relief. "Now we shan't have so much hard work with our feet."

She laughed almost gaily. "With mine, you mean!" she said. "Walking in this country doesn't seem to worry you much, Rex!"

"Used to it," he grunted.

Reaching the big saloon, they relaxed for a minute or two before carrying on. There was food and drink left ready for Brandon in the car, which he shared with the girl. Then they took up the trail once more, travelling more swiftly this time, though on several occasions Brandon was forced to leave the car and hack a way through denser undergrowth. It was simple enough to follow the track of Meyrick's trucks, and the two of them rocked and swayed along, in spite of the failing light.

It was almost dark when they came in sight of a glimmer of fire some distance in front. The next few minutes brought them to Meyrick's party, already encamped for the night.

"Stay in the car for a moment," said Brandon, getting out as Meyrick came across to greet him. The girl said nothing in reply, but settled in her seat.

"Surprise," said Brandon, as Meyrick peered inside the car suspiciously. "I've got a sort of hostage!"

"Holy smoke! Is that what you call her?" demanded Meyrick when he recognised Pierrette. "She's more like a permanent liability to my mind!"

Brandon opened the door for the girl, explaining how she came to be with him. Meyrick accepted the story without comment, but his interest quickened considerably when he heard all she had to tell as the three of them sat round the flap of his tent and had supper.

"So we can count on more trouble now that they've lost Pierrette," he mused when the tale was told. "Frankly, I don't mind a lot for myself, and

I reckon you can handle the Darracq man, Rex." He glanced at the girl. "As for Grier... I can't say. I know he's your uncle, Pierrette, but that doesn't make him any friend of mine. Sorry, but there it is."

She gave him an understanding smile. "I don't blame you, Mr. Meyrick," she said. "I've lost a lot of faith in uncle myself just recently. Don't let the fact of him being my uncle hinder your plans."

"Thank you," he answered gratefully. "I was afraid a somewhat difficult situation might arise in view of the circumstances, but you're being most co-operative."

"We push on at dawn, I take it," interposed Brandon.

Meyrick nodded agreement, lighting a cigarette as he did so. "By all means," he said. "Our objective is less than a week's trek distant now. The rock formation that you're interested in, Rex, is slightly closer. Unless the enemy delay us any more everything should be all right."

"Unless the enemy delay us…" murmured Brandon. "Yes, I see what you mean'!" He rose to his feet from the canvas chair in which he'd been sitting. Darkness enveloped the bush all around them. The glow of the fire was reflected in the glossy leaves of trees, overhead. Presently the moon would rise, cold and bright and silver. Brandon stood and gazed on the scene with unseeing eyes, his thoughts far away. Darracq would never take his beating lying down that was sure. They could expect some strong counter-move before many days were through. He decided to be on his guard all the time. And the girl must be watched as well. If Darracq could lay hands on her again it would suit him well, for he could use her safety as a threat to Brandon and Grier at the same time. Darracq had probably formed the wrong impression that she meant something to Brandon.

A mosquito pinged past his ear as he stood there, thinking. He brushed it away, turning abruptly.

"We should turn in," he said. "An early start in the morning, don't forget." They got up, saying goodnight.

Brandon took the girl to a third small tent which Llanga had pitched between his own and Meyrick's. At the entrance she turned and faced him.

"I'm glad I joined you," she told him simply.

"Early to tell yet," he answered. "You may regret it. Goodnight, Pierrette."

7

THE TERROR BY NIGHT

Next day the depleted party continued on its way. After the Durlenk attack there were only five bearers left, not counting Llanga, who brought the number up to six. Meyrick and Brandon travelled in the two trucks, battling a way through increasingly dense scrub and thorn jungle. It was plain that they would soon have to leave the vehicles to be picked up on the return trip, for there were many stretches where long detours were forced on the drivers.

Pierrette drove the big saloon, following the leading truck. With her was Llanga. The remaining five men were split up between the two trucks.

Progress that day was fair, considering the difficulties that confronted them. That night they camped on the bank of another river. Brandon strolled across to Meyrick as the latter was descending from his truck. Pierrette came to join the two men when she'd parked the car. She was hot and dusty. The last few miles had been trying in the extreme.

"I saw that aircraft of Gaynor's not an hour back," said Brandon. "Darracq's keeping an eye on us!"

Meyrick sniffed. "He'd drop a bomb on us if he had one, I expect," he grunted. "Come on, let's eat. We shall have to dispense with the vehicles tomorrow. The country gets more and more broken from here onwards."

Brandon looked at the rising hills towards which they'd been heading. He nodded. Dense jungle enveloped the hills as he stared at them in the gathering darkness. There was an eeriness about the scene that brought an unexpected shudder to his spine. He shook himself and helped with the unloading of the necessary gear for the night's camp. "There's one thing," he said to Pierrette presently when they were sitting down and relaxing.

"What's that, Rex?" she asked curiously.

"Moving through this country on foot with the small number of bearers we have left we shan't be such an obvious target to Darracq. In fact, I doubt if he'll be able to follow our route by spying from the air—if we take a few precautions."

"Something in that," chimed in Meyrick grimly. "We'll be burrowing through scrub and jungle like a lot of rabbits by noon tomorrow!"

Brandon sighed deeply. "What a prospect!" he said with a one-sided grin.

The girl laughed lightly. "I can take it if you can," she said. "I promised I wouldn't be a nuisance, didn't I?"

"You haven't been yet," he answered teasingly.

True to Meyrick's prophesy, the party were walking by midday after a few miles with the trucks. The vehicles themselves, and the car, were nosed into the bush and left to be picked up on the way back. Brandon thought the chances of Darracq finding them were slight, for they had been driven over a stretch of outcropping rock and shale, which hid their tracks effectively. Now they reposed in a narrow little clearing a full mile from their original line of advance.

Breaking off at a tangent, the safari continued in a northern direction. Meyrick took the lead, for he knew the country from previous trips. Brandon and the girl followed close behind him, while Llanga brought up the rear behind the remaining five men. They carried on in this manner for the rest of the day without undue incident. Towards evening Brandon was forced to use his rifle to bring down a rhinoceros which suddenly appeared in their path. The girl gave a gasp as she caught sight of the enormous armoured creature. It stood under a mchwili tree and gave a snorting squeal of rage at seeing the party. Some of the Shangaan bearers dropped their loads and scattered into the bush on either side of the narrow pathway they were following. Brandon thrust Pierrette behind him, while Meyrick brought up his rifle and aimed at the charging animal. Then Brandon fired a split second before his partner. Meyrick's shot rang out almost on top of Brandon's. The rhino staggered when it was halfway across the little clearing in which they had sighted it. Under the terrific impact of the two quick bullets it crumpled at the knees, somersaulting, tearing the earth up with its ploughing horn and coming to a dead halt not twenty yards from Meyrick and his companions.

Brandon whistled softly as he glanced at the girl. She was pale as she realised how nearly they had escaped.

Meyrick grinned cheerfully. "Nice shooting, the two of us!" he commented.

"I hope our shots weren't heard by Darracq," said Brandon shortly. "It'll give him a line on us if they are near enough to get the reports."

"Can't be helped," said Meyrick. "I refuse to be mown down by a charging rhino for the sake of silence!"

Brandon laughed softly. "Come on!" he said. "It's not be as bad as all that!" He shouted to the men, who reappeared somewhat sheepishly from the thick undergrowth into which they had fled in a body. Only Llanga had stood his ground while Brandon dealt with the threat of the rhino. Now he was grinning broadly, conscious of his own bravery, as much as the prowess of Brandon and Meyrick.

The girl, too, realised that her companions were both first class hunters when it came to speedy action; but she knew they would not look for praise from her. It was all a matter of course to them. To a woman, it was something different; something more powerful. She held her tongue, but her thoughts ran riot for a while.

The party pushed on without waste of time. If the shooting had been heard they did not want to hang around, but to put as much distance between themselves and Darracq as possible.

Once during the following day they heard, but did not see, the light aircraft. It seemed to be flying a long way to the south of where they were. Brandon was not lulled into full peace of mind by this; he thought it might all be a trap to make them think that Darracq had lost trace of them.

The country was worse than ever on this second day of the trek on foot. The ground was rising steeply now, with tangled jungle growth and thick scrub on all sides. Here and there rocky outcrops made the going harder still, but the party pressed on regardless of their increasing fatigue.

But, with nightfall, they made camp in a weary condition.

"This is more like a forced march than a hunting trip!" said Brandon to Meyrick. "Personally, I don't mind it all that much, but it must be pretty hard on Pierrette."

"I didn't ask her to come with us!" snapped Meyrick, who was himself feeling the strain. "You brought her along, don't forget!"

Brandon controlled his own frayed nerves, saving his temper by a narrow margin. "Forget it," he grunted. "I'm going to turn in as soon as I can."

"Sorry," said Meyrick. "I'm jagged, that's all."

"We'll both feel better in the morning."

Pierrette came up to them. "Now then, you two," she said, breaking in on their duet. "This is no time to start snapping and snarling at each other."

Brandon looked at her strangely. She was smiling as if there was nothing wrong; as if she had not walked miles that day in the torrid heat. He glanced at Meyrick, to see his partner grinning in an odd fashion.

"Seems as if she can take it better than we can!" said Meyrick ruefully. "Have to pull our socks up, Rex!"

"You're right there," agreed Brandon. "What about a bite to eat, eh?"

Harmony was restored. Both men realised it was through the influence of the girl. It gave them something of a jolt, but had a lasting effect on them.

The meal was finished when Llanga came silently up to Brandon and whispered in his ear.

Brandon stiffened. "What's that?" he demanded. "Something moving in the bush?"

Llanga glanced at Meyrick almost fearfully. "Yebbo, Inkosi," he murmured. "I do not know for sure, but I think it is men who make this sound. Many men, perhaps. Come!"

Brandon muttered something to Meyrick, then rose from his rhooki chair and sauntered indifferently out across the little patch of firelight around the camp fire.

He made for his tent, where he had left his rifles, and ducking inside brought out a medium-bore weapon with a full magazine. If Darracq should by any chance be snooping round the camp he meant to give him something to remember him by.

Then he strolled nonchalantly towards the spot indicated by Llanga.

Hardly had he crossed the clearing and reached the shadow of the mopani trees when there was a swift eruption of dusky figures. Wild whoops and yells rent the air as an avalanche of spear-carrying savages burst into view.

Brandon dropped to one knee, firing as he went down. He had not expected an attack from blacks, but his actions were so swift and automatic that he was shooting before he had time to take in the general situation. Behind him he heard other sounds of battle. The Shangaans were scattered in a moment. He knew that Meyrick would not have had time to grab a gun from where he was sitting. The thought worried him considerably. Pierrette might run for it, but there was the possibility that the camp was surrounded by the savages. Brandon did not even know who they were, or to what tribe they belonged. Meyrick had said nothing of hostile natives when they entered the immediate district.

The savages were sweeping towards him, hurling their spears and throwing clubs. Then an arrow whistled past his head and plunged into the ground close behind him. He fired again and again, bringing down several of the attackers in quick succession. But as yet his was the only gun in camp that spat death. And he was vastly outnumbered by the savages.

Still firing with a calmness that would have surprised even himself had he been conscious of it, he was overwhelmed, borne backwards in the tide of sweating humanity that engulfed him. The last thing he remembered was the fanatical face of a towering black man with white beads round his neck. Then everything went dark as something crashed on his skull in a shower of stars and dazzling lights that blinded him.

Faintly to his ears came the shouting and the clamour of a mob run wild. He thought he heard a scream that might have been that of a woman in terror, then silence fell in the world of darkness in which he swayed and sank.

There is something hideously unnatural about the thoughts which run through a man's mind when he is returning from the black world of unconsciousness. Brilliant light seemed to sear his eyes when he opened them, but he could see nothing that was tangible. There was a humming in his ears and a throb at the back of his head that was neither pain nor sound, but a mixture of both. Instinctively he tried to move his head. Darting specks of flame shot out across his eyes so that he froze into still rigidity again. Gradually the agony and numbness faded. He began to pick out different noises from the background of sound inside his buzzing head. He thought he heard a distinct voice speaking not far away. There was a faintly familiar note about it, but for the life of him he could not lay a finger on where he had heard it before.

Then the voice was closer, almost directly over him, it seemed. He tried to open his eyes again. The lids refused to part at first. A great weight settled on his forehead and felt as if it was pressing him down into the ground. He forced himself to move; even a little would be better than nothing.

Then the voice in his ears was suddenly clear and lucid. "Time this Brandon fellow showed some life," said the voice. "Hey, Meeba, bring water!"

Brandon lay still, trying to understand the significance of the remark. It took a long time to sink in. Then a swift rush of cold water doused his head and chest before he had a chance of fully realising what was happening.

He opened his eyes abruptly, shocked by the sudden impact of the cold water. Broad daylight greeted him, making him blink painfully. The shock of the water made him gasp for breath. He tried to move and found that something was holding his wrists and legs. With a grim sort of reaction he began to understand.

Through the haze that danced before his eyes he saw the tall thin form of Darracq standing over him, a revolver in his hand. Beside Darracq was the grinning face of a native. The bearer still held a canvas bucket in one hand; water slopped from its brim as he moved.

"So you're awake!" sneered Darracq. "It's about time, too! What happened here in the night?"

"I thought you'd know all about it," retorted Brandon. He was feeling a little stronger by this time; strong enough, to find out that his hands and feet were securely tied.

"I'm as much in the dark as you seem to be," answered the other man. "We followed you up and found you an hour ago. There's one dead

Shangaan, one wounded and yourself. No sign of Meyrick or the girl you abducted, but you seem to have killed about half a dozen natives before they got you down."

"Glad to hear it!" grunted Brandon tersely. "I don't know any more than you do about the natives. They jumped us a while after nightfall." He was conscious of a sick sense of failure when Darracq mentioned Meyrick and Pierrette.

"Jumped you!" snarled Darracq. "That's just the sort of fool thing I'd have expected to happen to you! Now it looks as if we've got to find Meyrick again before we get our hands on the ivory."

"You mean they're prisoners of the savages?" Darracq laughed bleakly. "Bit slow on the uptake this morning, aren't you?" he sneered. "Of course they are! They wouldn't have run out and left you, would they? And they certainly aren't around here."

Brandon absorbed the information grimly, "What happened then?" he demanded. "Let me loose and I'll find them!"

Darracq didn't answer; instead he kicked Brandon hard in the ribs and turned on his heel, yelling for some of the natives.

"Take him back to the camp!" ordered Darracq, jerking his head at Brandon. "If he gets away I'll flay the skin off your backs!"

Brandon was dragged to his feet. He saw Darracq still wandering round the desolated camp, searching for clues. Then he was forced to stand while his legs were freed. A rope was attached to his wrists and held by three of Darracq's men. A few minutes later he was being marched southward through the jungle, making for the camp established by Darracq and Grier. It was less than a couple of miles away, but Brandon was feeling the strain by the time he arrived within sight of it. His head ached fit to burst and his knees felt weak as water. Nor did the blacks spare him anything in their determination to carry out their master's orders to the letter.

When the party arrived at the camp they were greeted by Grier. The man stared in amazement at sight of Brandon and his manner of arrival. Certainly he had not expected any such thing as a prisoner to be delivered.

Brandon said: "You're a fool, Grier! If you had the smallest speck of sense in your head you'd turn me loose and let me get after Darracq. And you'd get out of this as fast as you could for your own sake!"

Grier shifted nervously from one foot to the other as he gaped at Brandon uneasily.

"You know I can't do that," he said peevishly. "What's happened to Pierrette? Where's Darracq?"

"Answer your own questions, you fool!" snapped Brandon. His nerves were taut strung as he gazed round the camp. The site chosen was a large clearing with a reasonably level floor. Partly hidden by trees on the far side was the light aircraft.

Gricr took a grip on himself, turning unpleasant in his weakness and spite. He ordered Brandon to be put in one of the three tents that stood nearby. The bearers did as they were ordered. "Tie his legs again!" added Grier. "When Darracq returns he will know how to treat you, Brandon! This is a monstrous thing. You seized my niece, and if Darracq doesn't bring her back with him I shall hold you responsible for her disappearance."

Brandon didn't deign to answer. He was wondering where Jerry Gaynor, the pilot, was. There was no sign of him about the camp. Perhaps he was away for a time, out with a gun, maybe. Surely, he thought to himself, Gaynor must realise by this time what was going on? He wasn't the type of man to stand by and do nothing.

As if in answer to his unspoken questions Grier called after him: "You'll have company in there, Brandon! There's another righteous idiot we've had to put under guard. He didn't like our methods when he learnt about them!"

Brandon glanced round, but Grier was standing some way off, watching him uneasily.

The tent fly was thrown open by one of the blacks as Brandon was thrust inside. An armed bearer stood nearby, his rifle slung military fashion from his glistening shoulder.

Inside the tent Brandon was tripped and thrown to the ground, while one of the 'boys' lashed his legs together. He became aware of someone else on the ground close to him. It was Jerry Gaynor, but the young man said nothing while the natives were there with them. Only when they were left on their own did he speak, and then it was with a rueful grin.

"So they caught up with you at last, eh?" he muttered in a whisper.

"I'm sorry, Brandon. Didn't think they'd put it over you so easily."

"They didn't!" answered Brandon. "We were attacked by hostile savages. Pierrette and my partner, Meyrick, were captured. Most of our men were killed; the rest fled. Darracq came and found me while I was still unconscious."

"I see," said Gaynor grimly. "So that's the way of it, eh? I didn't know, of course. They've kept me a prisoner for three days now—ever since I said what I thought of their hunting methods after learning a bit about what they were up to. I'm sorry about Pierrette, though. She had no hand in it."

"She ran away from Darracq," answered Brandon briefly.

"What are we going to do?"

"Get out of here as soon as we can and go after the girl and Meyrick. With any luck we shall be able to trail the savages who took them. Darracq, I imagine, is doing the same right now. I'd like to get ahead of him."

Gaynor was silent for a moment. Then: "Look," he said quietly, "I've been working on my bonds for quite a while now. They aren't very secure. With any luck we can free ourselves and make a break, but I suggest we wait till nightfall."

"That would certainly increase the chances," agreed Brandon slowly. "It'll give Darracq more time, of course, but I think you're right. We'll hang on here; Darracq won't be back yet-awhile in any event." He paused. "Have you a gun of any kind?" he added thoughtfully.

"There's a Colt automatic in my tent over there. We may be able to get it before we leave."

Brandon grunted in a satisfied manner. His head was still singing, but it did not feel so sore as it had done a while ago. But he was worried about Meyrick and the girl.

The hours seemed to drag interminably, but at length the shadows outside the tent in which they were tied up lengthened and grew darker. The slit of daylight they could see through the laced fly slowly faded into purple gloom. The heat inside the tent, which during the day had been intense, gradually lessened, so that both men felt relief from the stifling sensation of being shut in an oven.

"Won't be long now," murmured Brandon. "How have you fared with your bonds? Are they loose enough to slip out of yet? Mine haven't responded, I'm afraid. You'll have to untie me when you're free yourself. Those devils made a good job of me!"

Gaynor said nothing for a moment, then he grunted in a way that was almost cheerful.

"Any minute now!" he whispered. "Grier will change the sentry on duty outside in just about fifteen minutes. As soon as they're finished we'll make a break. O.K.?"

"Suits me," muttered Brandon.

They waited in absolute silence, listening with every nerve on the alert. Presently there were voices, sounds of movement. A minute afterwards Gaynor was sitting up, free.

8

THE ELEPHANT GOD

FULL DARKNESS had come to the jungle by the time Gaynor was free of his bonds and releasing Brandon. The two of them paused and listened carefully before making the next move. Then Brandon lifted the canvas of the tent at the rear, where he knew it backed almost on to the fringe of undergrowth round the clearing where the camp was placed. Lying flat on his stomach, he peered beneath the canvas, seeing only darkness. From the tent fly itself, they could see the glow of fires and the shadowy figures of bearers squatting round them. The smell of cooking reached their nostrils, reminding them that they had not eaten that day at all. One of the blacks was sitting with his back to the tent fly, not a yard away.

"Come on," breathed Brandon. "We'll get out the back and work our way to the rear of your old tent. A gun would be very useful if you can get it."

Gaynor grinned in the darkness. Then they were worming their way beneath the back of the tent, free men.

The escape worked out better than Brandon had dared to hope. Jerry Gaynor had less difficulty in getting his gun than he had experienced in freeing himself, and now the pair of fugitives were slipping through the dense jungle growth as fast as their legs would carry them. Despite the speed at which they moved neither man made a noise.

Not until they had covered nearly a mile did Brandon pause to pick up his direction more exactly. Then they were off again, speaking little.

With the coming of dawn progress improved. They were now well past the neighbourhood of Meyrick's last camp where the attack had taken place. Brandon had picked a jungle path at random and used it to take them northward in the general direction from which he thought the savages had come.

In daylight they could see the rising crest of a sugar-loaf hill in the distance. It stood out above the more gradually sloping hills, and seemed to act as a sign-post. Working as much on instinct as any other sense, Brandon kept pressing forward. He did not know for certain where the prisoners had been taken, and he did not know how far in advance of them Darracq might be.

Sometime before noon they had a stroke of luck. The path they were following was joined by another coming in at an angle. Brandon paused and bent to examine the ground. As he did so Gaynor gripped his shoulder and pointed. Further along the path something was lying on the ground. Brandon saw it was a revolver, and when Gaynor picked it up he recognised it as Meyrick's.

"They must have been brought this way!" he muttered in an elated whisper of triumph.

Breaking the revolver, he saw that all the shots had been fired. Presumably Meyrick had managed to retain it when he and the girl were captured. Now it came to Brandon. Fortunately he found that there were still a handful of cartridges to fit it in his bush shirt pocket.

They now had a definite trail to follow, for no attempt had been made by the savages to hide their trail. Since they had been using a path beaten through the jungle, Brandon and Gaynor had little difficulty in speeding up their movements.

"You know what?" said Gaynor breathlessly. "It looks as if Darracq couldn't have come this way. If he and his men had been on this trail they wouldn't have left that gun on the ground. And they couldn't very well have missed it."

"Maybe they lost the trail earlier on," grunted Brandon. "Let's hope they did. I'd hate to arrive to find that Darracq had beaten us to it and captured Pierrette and Meyrick himself!"

The path was leading them directly to the sugar-loaf hill now. The afternoon wore on with monotonous heat and the irritating attacks of a myriad of insects. Both men were tired and hungry by this time, but nothing would have slowed them down.

Darkness was falling swiftly as they climbed the lower slopes of the sugar-loaf hill. They slowed their advance a little, moving with greater caution. Then Brandon came to an abrupt halt, head thrown back, as he listened. Every nerve in his hardened body was tingling. His ears had not deceived him. From no great distance there came the throb of a muted drum, the mutter of many voices raised in some form of chant.

He exchanged a glance with Raynor. "That'll be them, all right!" he whispered with conviction. "Come on!"

"Round the side of the hill," said Gaynor. "That's where the sound comes from, Rex!"

Brandon nodded quickly. "Right again!" he breathed. They worked round the shoulder of the hillside. The scene that confronted them after another quarter of an hour was one which brought their hearts to their mouths and sent them grabbing for the guns they carried. But Brandon knew there was nothing they could do from this distance. He let out a whispered oath and touched Gaynor's sleeve. They moved on more swiftly.

Slightly lower down the hillside than the line they were following was a sort of cup in the ground. It formed a basin in the side of the hill, sheltering a native village and acting as a natural amphitheatre for the grim scene of barbarism now taking place before their eyes. The beat of the drums was louder; the chanting of a hundred voices rose stridently. Firelight glowed bright and flickering, casting shadows that might have been part of a fantastic stage set had it not been for the grotesque setting and the human characters who played out the drama.

"My God!" breathed Gaynor. "They've got the girl and your partner. What the devil's going on?"

Brandon stared hard at the enormous shape of a statue that reared up at the back end of the basin. It was in the form of the head of an elephant, but it was several times life-size. The dancing flames made it appear alive.

"The Elephant God!" murmured Brandon. "I've heard stories of this cult, but never seen it in action before."

In front of the massive idol were two tall wooden stakes standing upright in the ground. To each one a white figure was lashed. Brandon guessed who the people were, but it was not for a moment or two that he realised how desperate their plight was.

Piles of brush wood, and scrub were stacked round their feet. They would shortly be burnt alive, sacrificed to the dreadful Elephant God of the savages. Even now, the beating of the drums and the singing of the wildly gesticulating natives was reaching fever pitch. Weaving in a wide belt between the idol and the prisoners, dancing madly, were many black-skinned forms. Between Brandon and the prisoners were hundreds of savages, sitting or standing, swaying in time to the music of the drums and the singing voices. One of the dancing men was darting to and fro with a lighted torch in his hand, waving it aloft, sweeping the ground with it, each movement bringing it gradually closer and closer to the two prisoners at the stakes.

"I can't stand this!" gasped Gaynor. "That girl..."

"Steady!" snapped Brandon in a whisper. "We've got to get nearer before we act."

They started forward, Brandon leading the way, his eyes resting on the image of the Elephant God with a sort of grim thoughtfulness. A vague plan was already forming in his fertile brain. It was perfectly obvious that the two of them could not hope to launch an attack on the savages and get away with it. The odds were enormous. Something a little more subtle was needed.

When they had crawled to within twenty yards of the crowd of natives Brandon stopped and whispered in Gaynor's ear. The pilot nodded briefly as he listened. "Good luck!" he muttered.

Brandon melted away in the darkness, invisible beyond the circle of firelight thrown upwards from the centre of the basin. There was no time to lose, yet he could not afford to give himself away at this critical stage. The life of the girl and his partner might well hang on what he did in the next few minutes.

Gaynor slithered across the uneven ground into a better position. He was as close to the captives as he could get without being visible to the savages, and now there was nothing he could do until Brandon gave a sign.

The suspense of waiting strained his nerves to breaking point, but somehow or other he forced himself to lie there and watch as the madly whirling witch doctor with the torch went nearer and nearer to the prisoners.

Even from that distance Gaynor could see the look of anguish and fear on Pierrette's drawn face. Meyrick stared fixedly in front of him, his whole demeanour revealing him as a solid, stubborn man. Once he turned his head a little and spoke to the girl. Gaynor guessed it was a word of encouragement.

The drums and the chanting grew wilder and wilder. Then the witch doctor, who seemed to be in charge of the proceedings, came to a quivering halt in front of the idol statue, his flaming torch held high in the air as he sank to his knees and brought his face down to the ground. The chanting ceased abruptly, as did the drums. In the utter silence Gaynor heard the crackle of the fires. Then the witch doctor called out something in a high-pitched, crazy voice. It sounded like a question.

Whether it was a question or not Gaynor never really knew, but the next development brought the most unexpected effect he had ever imagined.

From the raised trunk and mouth of the grotesque Elephant God there was emitted the unmistakable bellow of a tusker on the rampage. It squealed long and loud, the hideous sound echoing back and forth from the hillside above the cup.

For an instant nothing happened. The entire gathering seemed momentarily frozen with superstitious terror as they listened to the voice of their God. Gaynor felt a wild excitement sweeping over him as he tensed himself for action. This was the sign Brandon had promised him. Next instant the full effect of the eerie voice of the statue was revealed. With a thin wail of fear the savages rose to their feet as one. Gaynor could hardly believe his eyes. The savages turned and fled from the basin in a body, leaving only the witch doctor where he had been prostrating himself in front of the idol.

Wailing and gibbering among themselves, the wild-eyed natives broke completely. In a few seconds there was no one on the scene but the witch doctor and the two prisoners.

Gaynor leapt to his feet, his automatic gripped in his hand as he darted towards the two captives. The witch doctor saw him coming. Of all the tribe, the hideously-painted savage had the sense to realise that the bellow of the Elephant God was a fake. Its trumpet of anger must be in some way connected with this white man. He rushed at the stake to which the girl was tied, reaching it a few feet in advance of Gaynor. Meyrick yelled a warning. The witch doctor brandished his flaming torch and touched it to the brushwood at the base of the stake.

Instantly flames leapt upwards around the helpless girl. She cried out in fear. Then Gaynor fired at the savage, dropping him like a stone, his head in the fire he had started. There was a long-bladed knife thrust into the man's loin cloth. Gaynor bent and whipped it out, slashing at the cords that secured the girl. Pierrette struggled free, kicking the flaming brands aside as she staggered clear of the fire. Her fair hair was scorched and the white shirt she wore was blackened by smoke. Otherwise she seemed to be unhurt.

Gaynor said something to her and raced for Meyrick. Almost at the same time the figure of Rex Brandon appeared from behind the Elephant God statue. He sprinted towards them, revolver in hand. Seeing that Gaynor was dealing with Meyrick satisfactorily, he gripped Pierrette by the wrist and hurried her to the edge of the jungle. Gaynor and Meyrick were not slow to follow. Within a matter of three or four minutes from the time of the Elephant God's trumpet, the two prisoners and their rescuers were racing through the dense undergrowth, fully aware that pursuit would begin the moment the warriors realised how they'd been fooled.

"How on earth did you manage it?" gasped Pierrette.

Brandon grinned in the darkness. "I'd heard tales of these Elephant Gods," he explained. "Knew a man who'd seen one and described it. They're made of skin and a wooden framework, and they don't usually play a speaking part! All I did was to sneak round and get inside the fake head. The rest was easy. I can imitate an elephant any time!"

"Lucky for us you can," she answered. They hurried on, penetrating deeper and deeper into the jungle that clothed the sides of the sugar-loaf hill. Not till the first flush of dawn was tinting the sky did they slacken their pace and halt. There was no sign of the pursuit they fully expected. To all intents and purpose they were alone in the stillness of the jungle, with only the birds and small animals of the wild for company.

Meyrick was showing traces of great excitement, his eyes darting this way and that as he studied their immediate surroundings.

"Something on your mind?" queried Brandon. "We're close to the place I was aiming to reach," said his partner. "As far as I can remember the graveyard lies on the far side of this curious hill, right at the bottom of the slopes. It's well hidden from all round."

Brandon nodded thoughtfully. "Apparently the local tribe hold the district in some veneration," he mused. "The odds are that they never venture into the graveyard itself. If we can locate it exactly it will do for a perfect hiding place till we're properly organised again."

"What about the ivory?" demand Meyrick excitedly. Brandon smiled reassuringly. "We'll kill two birds with one stone," he said. "Finding the elephants' graveyard will give us the white gold, as well as securing our position. But we can't expect to take away much of value on our own. And don't forget that Darracq and his gang are still around somewhere! We can't discount them. Even if we could carry off as much of the white gold as we wanted to—which we obviously can't at this stage—there'd be no guarantee that Darracq wouldn't take it off us. He has a far stronger force than we have, remember; we've only two pistols between us, which isn't much if it came to a pitched battle."

"All the same," protested Meyrick, "we'll make for the graveyard and see what happens. I know my way from here."

"Lead on, in that case," said Brandon. "I wish we had some food. None of us has eaten for about thirty-six hours to my knowledge." He looked about him, sighting a cluster of wild fruit hanging from the lower branches of a tree. They tasted sour when he picked them, but they were better than nothing. Any more solid food was out of the question at the moment. They dare not light a fire, even if they had had the food to cook on it.

Pressing on again, Meyrick followed a jungle path with all the certainty of a man who knows where he's going. His one and only aim was to set eyes on the long and naturally-hoarded white gold again. He realised they would not be able to take away the spoils; but there was nothing to stop them looking.

Brandon followed cheerfully enough. But his interest in the white gold was far more academic than Meyrick's. He wanted, too, to examine the chromic-ferrous deposits which were supposed to be nearby the elephants' graveyard. As for the ivory, he would willingly partner Meyrick in realising its value, but until they could return with a strong force of 'boys' there was little chance of that. At best they could only succeed in preventing Darracq and Grier from getting it ahead of them. That in itself would be quite a difficult achievement under the circumstances. "It's only a mile or two further on!" said Meyrick with increasing excitement. He was behaving like a schoolboy by this time, fairly dancing at the prospect of showing his companions the age-long wealth that centuries had stored for the man who found it.

"Good," grunted Brandon a little absent-mindedly. He was wondering what had become of Darracq, and whether they would run into the man unexpectedly. If they did things might not be so funny, for Darracq would certainly be out to get them. Darracq had struck Brandon as a singularly vindictive person.

The path they followed skirted the thick upper limits of the jungle cloaking the sugar-loaf hill. By this time they were right round on the opposite side to the place where the savages had held their sacrificial ceremony.

Meyrick halted for a moment, thinking, recalling the way and the lie of the land. "We go down a bit here/' he said, presently. "I think the graveyard is there, somewhere in that mass of forest land yonder." He pointed with his hand.

"Lead on," said Gaynor cheerfully. "We'll follow."

Pierrette smiled at him. She had a very great regard for Jerry Gaynor, and the fact that the pilot had rescued her when the flames were licking her feet, only went to deepen her feelings.

Brandon, close on the heels of Meyrick, grinned to himself. His eyes were searching the ground for spoor of animals or men. The last thing he wanted to do was walk into Darracq's arms when he wasn't prepared for it. But he did not see the tracks of men, black or white. Instead, he caught sight of broken branches ahead. Something large had brushed through the edge of the trees. His eyes dropped to the ground again. He touched Meyrick on the shoulder.

"Look," he said, quietly. "Elephant!"

They halted, staring at the great round tracks. A big elephant had joined the narrow jungle path, going in the same direction as themselves. Wordlessly they looked at each other, then Brandon jerked his head.

"The graveyard," he said. "It's heading that way."

9

MAN AGAINST MONSTER

"Do you mean to tell me that these tracks belong to an elephant on its way to this graveyard?" said Gaynor in a tone of incredulity.

Brandon shrugged. "I should think it's quite likely," he replied. "From stories one hears elephants normally avoid the neighbourhood of a place like this, coming to it only when they are close to death. It's all a matter of guesswork, naturally, because, to the best of my knowledge, no man has ever discovered one of these graveyards before."

"Well," said Pierrette, slowly, "if this animal is on its way to die it'll show us the right path, I suppose. Is it safe to follow it, Rex?"

Brandon examined the spoor. From what he could tell the elephant, which, from its tracks, was an enormous one, was moving slowly, probably limping along. The tracks were not many hours old, in fact, from what Brandon read in the sign, they might even be more recent than that. He paused in his stride, listening closely for any sound that would indicate the creature was nearer than he expected.

Only the multitude of bird song reached his ears. "Come on," he said quietly. "We can't hang around and wait for something to happen."

In silence, conscious of a fresh sense of danger in the air, the party advanced.

Brandon realised only too well that they were not equipped to fight even a wounded elephant. Had he had a rifle with him he would not have been so anxious, but one automatic and one revolver were poor weapons indeed if it came to a pinch.

The path dropped now, descending the side of the slope at a much steeper angle. Dense mchwili and mopani trees pressed in on both sides, limiting their view ahead to a matter of yards only. The undergrowth of scrub and thorn bush made things even worse. And there was always the danger that their enemies, the savages who worshipped the Elephant God, might be anywhere at hand. There was also the risk that Darracq was lurking in the neighbourhood, though Brandon had come to the conclusion that the man had probably returned to Grier's camp for reinforcements and a new move.

The elephant was still moving in front of them somewhere. Its tracks were fresh, but showed that the creature was badly sick or wounded. Suddenly, the tall growths of mopani trees thinned out at the edge of a small clearing. The path widened out, opening into a broad shelf of land that was cut by the elements into the side of the age-old hill.

Brandon paused, listening and peering round with inborn caution.

The spoor of the elephant crossed the little clearing in a zig-zag course. It disappeared into the scrub on the far side, where the path was resumed.

"All right," breathed Brandon tensely. "Come on, everyone. I think it's safe, but keep your eyes peeled."

Without a word they started again.

Halfway across the clearing Pierrette gave a strangled gasp. At the same instant there was a crashing sound in the thickets ahead. Brandon and Meyrick halted in their tracks, staring at the moving undergrowth. Then Meyrick cursed savagely and grabbed at Gaynor's automatic.

"Back!" he yelled. "It's going to charge us!"

Brandon stood his ground, jaw thrust out grimly. He knew there was no time to reach the cover from which they had come.

"Run for it!" he shouted to Meyrick and the other two.

The great grey hulk of a savage old elephant broke into view, ears outstretched, trunk raised, as it suddenly squealed its challenge to the puny men who dared to disturb its last lone journey by trailing it.

Brandon levelled his revolver. The elephant rushed towards him at a staggering run, trumpeting angrily. Despite its age and illness it came with the speed of an express train, its enormous feet making the very ground shake with their every impact.

Meyrick and the others scattered. From the corner of his eye Brandon saw that Gaynor was getting the girl out of harm's way. Meyrick halted when he had covered a few yards and turned again, firing the automatic wildly in a vain attempt to stop the charging elephant. But Brandon held his fire. He knew that nothing but a close shot would stop the beast, and even then it would be a case of touch and go.

The great animal was close to him now, bearing down on him, its small eyes red with fury and sickness.

He levelled the revolver and fired, aiming at the brute's open mouth. The only result was a scream of rage and pain more frightful than its previous cries. Then it was on top of him.

Brandon hurled himself aside, but the move was a fraction of a second too late. Before he realised what was going to happen he felt himself seized round the waist in a grip of steel and lifted from the ground as if he had weighed next to nothing.

Half crushed in the terrible embrace of the elephant's trunk he managed to retain his rigid self-discipline, refusing to give way to the swift fear that threatened to swallow him.

The breath of the furious animal was hot and fetid on his face. At any moment he expected to be hurled to the ground and trampled to death in an instant of time. If he was to save himself from that fate he must act quickly and coolly. All these thoughts ran through his lightning brain during the uncountable seconds in which he felt himself whirled aloft.

He still gripped his revolver, and the hand that held it was steady and free. Fighting to drown the instinctive fear that seized him, he brought the gun round and aimed it straight at the elephant's right eye, only inches from his own.

The shock of the report and the impact of the heavy leaden bullet were so great that for a moment he thought the end of the world had come. There was blood spurting from the creature's eye, but its grip on his body seemed to tighten instead of relaxing. He fired again in the same spot, knowing that his life was forfeit if he failed to kill the monster animal that held him high in the air. The elephant gave a rumbling groan as the revolver kicked in Brandon's hand. Then he suddenly felt himself falling as the thick trunk uncurled. The creature was dying. Brandon hit the ground with a thud that almost-winded him. Staring upwards for a split second he saw the toppling mountain of grey flesh above him. From what seemed a great distance Pierrette cried a desperate warning. He struggled to move quickly enough to avoid the staggering, falling bulk of the elephant. It stood close above him now, swaying blindly, buckling at the knees.

Only by a tremendous effort did Brandon force himself to move. The elephant began to fall forwards. Someone seized Brandon by the leg and dragged him violently backwards. At the same time the carcase of the elephant hit the ground with a shuddering crash, narrowly missing his head. He rolled clear and sat up straight, leaping to his feet almost before the great quivering body had come to rest.

"My God," muttered Meyrick close to his side, "I hope I never live to see anything like that again. Put the wind up me that time!"

"You're not the only one," answered Brandon grimly. He looked round, seeing Pierrette and Gaynor running towards them across the clearing. Gaynor looked uncomfortable.

"I was a coward to run like that," he said.

"You'd have been in the way if you'd stuck around," said Brandon with a grin. "Besides, you got the girl away."

Gaynor still seemed uneasy. They all stood looking at the monstrous carcase of the dead elephant. Its grey bulk seemed to fill the clearing in which they stood. Then Brandon snapped out of his brief reverie.

"We must move fast now!" he said grimly. "That shooting could have been heard a long way off. Before we know where we are we'll have the black devils on our track—to say nothing of Darracq and Grier."

Meyrick nodded briefly. "You're right!" he grunted.

Brandon was still a bit shaken from his recent experience, but he started off across the clearing, leading his companions onwards again. He noticed that the girl eyed him with a look of open admiration in her eyes. She said nothing, but her look was eloquent. Gaynor, too, was obviously much impressed by Brandon's exhibition of courage in his life and death battle with the sick elephant. Few men could have fought such a battle and survived. But Rex Brandon was not as other men. His comrades seemed to sense it and respect him the more because of it.

The path dropped even more steeply now, burrowing through almost impenetrable undergrowth, so that the party had to push their way through a tangle of liana and thorn. Their clothes were torn and ragged by the time they emerged on the brink of what at first seemed to be a sheer drop. Then Brandon saw that the path angled away to the left, skirting the drop in the side of the hill.

Meyrick caught Brandon's arm, pointing down the hill to the densest part of the jungle below.

"That's where it is," he said quietly, his voice tense with excitement. "Down there, Rex!"

"So I gather," said Brandon dryly. "It'll serve us as a hiding place till things quieten down, but you can't expect to carry off your white gold this time, you know? "

Meyrick's face grew serious instantly. "I realise that," he replied in a hurried whisper. "But there's something about the thought of all that wealth lying there just waiting to be collected."

Brandon grinned. "Gets under your skin, doesn't it?" he murmured. "Well, we'll see, but don't bank on anything this trip."

Meyrick understood and nodded agreement. "I'm quite prepared to wait for another opportunity," he answered. "It's just that I'd hate Darracq to lay his hands on the stuff before we do.

"We'll be waiting for him if we lie up in the graveyard itself," said Gaynor grimly. "Personally, I wouldn't turn a hair if neither of them left the jungle alive." He shot a glance at the girl who was walking at his side. "Sorry, Pierrette, but I don't much care for your uncle — any more than I do for Darracq."

"You don't have to apologise," she said. "I've lost all the respect I ever had for him. He's weak, with an underlying streak of badness that ruins him."

Gaynor seemed a little relieved by what she said. They went on in silence, dropping down the side of the hill towards the deep, scrub-choked hollow that formed the elephants' graveyard.

Presently Meyrick called Brandon's attention to a large amount of outcropping rock to one side of the path.

"It's hereabouts that the biggest deposits of your chromic-ferrous rock formations are," he said.

Brandon's interest quickened as he scanned the immediate surroundings. Partly hidden in the undergrowth were big shelving ridges of stone, streaked with purple-red -and flecked with green—the tell-tale chromic-ferrous strata. Brandon halted and made a closer examination of the colourful rock. He knew then that he was to be rewarded by the discovery, no matter what happened regarding the other objects of the safari. The rock formation was certainly chromic-ferrous in nature, and it looked as if it was exceptionally rich.

"This is worth coming all the way to see," he said at length. "I shall owe you a lot, Meyrick, by the time we get back home." His eyes were bright as he spoke, for the geologist in him was uppermost for the moment. All other considerations were submerged by his latest discovery.

"You're welcome," said Meyrick cheerfully. "All I ask in return is your help in getting the white gold back to civilisation. Not this time, of course, but later on.'.'

"You have my word on that," answered Brandon firmly.

Meyrick opened his mouth to say something more when he suddenly stopped, turning his head abruptly and peering into the thick brush that pressed in on them from all sides. Brandon, too, had heard the stealthy sound. Instantly he forgot every sentence about his geological find, returning to the business in hand with renewed determination, every nerve on the alert as he listened.

There was no sound now in the stillness that engulfed the jungle pathway on which they stood.

"Could have been nothing but an animal," whispered Gaynor.

Brandon shook his head uneasily. "Could have been," he muttered. "All the same—" With a movement so fast that it was almost impossible to follow, he threw himself aside as the foliage parted and a spear whistled through the air and buried itself in the bole of a mchwili tree. Had Brandon not moved when he did he would have been struck.

"Down!" he yelled. "We're attacked!" As he spoke the undergrowth was violently disturbed. Tall, menacing figures broke into view. Spears were thrown. Brandon ducked as a throwing club passed over his head. He and Meyrick were firing as the warriors launched themselves. Several of them dropped in their tracks, wild battle cries on their lips. It was then that Brandon caught a glimpse of a white man in the rear of the natives. It was Grier, and he carried a rifle, urging the attackers on to capture or kill the fugitives. Seeing Pierrette he yelled something about the girl, but the heat of the battle grew so intense that Brandon lost the actual words.

Falling back in the face of the savage attack, Brandon and his companions found themselves scrambling over the strata of chromic-ferrous rock at their backs. Dropping on the far side of a ridge of the stuff, Brandon used it as a sort of breastwork, firing the revolver from behind its cover. He counted his shots carefully, knowing that ammunition was limited. Meyrick had had some more cartridges in his pocket and Brandon had reloaded the revolver after killing the elephant. Now there were two shots left in his gun. He used one of them to send Grier scuttling out of sight among the thorn scrub, then decided the time had come to beat a retreat.

"Back through the rocks!" he called to Meyrick and the other two. Pierrette was already crouching down behind the scanty cover they had found. Gaynor, unarmed and helpless to assist his companions, shielded her as best he could. He wrenched a spear from where it quivered in a tree and hurled it back at the enemy, scoring a hit more by luck than judgment.

They slithered further in among the outcrops of stratified rock, looking this way and that for better cover. Brandon was afraid they would be taken from the rear and surrounded, but luck was with them for the time being.

The natives launched a more determined attack, leaping over the rocks regardless of their casualties, as Meyrick fired Gaynor's automatic with deadly effect. Not a bullet was wasted. Gaynor brought a spare clip of ammunition from his pocket and tossed it across to Meyrick when the automatic ran out. Brandon, meanwhile, had reloaded his revolver. He covered Meyrick while the latter pushed home the fresh clip and took up the fight again. Between them they held the attackers at bay, giving Gaynor and the girl an opportunity to search for better quarters than their present ones.

Suddenly Gaynor called to Brandon from some distance off. There was a note of excitement in his voice. "Here!" he shouted. "Quick; this is just what we want."

Brandon wasted no time in leaping to his feet and leading Meyrick through the rocks and tangled undergrowth. They found Gaynor and Pierrette standing close against the edge of a deep hole that burrowed into the ground between two large piles of rock. It disappeared at an angle, forming a sort of cave large enough for a man to crawl through.

"That'll do!" snapped Brandon, glancing over, his shoulder. There was no sign of the warriors for the moment. Either they were regrouping for another assault, or Grier had called them off for a time until he knew what was going to happen to Pierrette. Perhaps he had not expected the Elephant God worshippers to take things quite so much into their own hands. His object had plainly been to capture, not kill, his rivals.

However, whichever way it was, there was no time to lose. Brandon ducked into the mouth of the little cave and sniffed. The air reeked of decaying flesh. A faint breeze seemed to strike his cheek as he crawled in through the opening. The others followed him closely, Meyrick bringing up the rear with a whispered word that the savages were still out of sight.

They were a few yards inside the little cave in the ground when clearly from outside came the sound of voices calling to one another.

"No noise!" hissed Brandon. He turned and wriggled back towards the mouth of the cave, peering through it at the green curtain of foliage that closed in around its opening. Several of the natives were in sight now, bending to examine the ground. They seemed at a loss as to where the fugitives had disappeared to. Then Grier walked forward, his rifle held rigidly in his hands, staring this way and that in an effort to locate them. Hardly daring to breathe, the little party crouched in their hole in the ground and watched, expecting at any moment to hear the yell of triumph that would greet discovery of their hiding place.

But it was not a cry of triumph that broke the silence of the jungle.

Nor did it come from above ground. Instead, there was a sudden growling roar from somewhere deep inside the cave, behind them. Brandon caught his breath and cursed. The smell of decaying flesh should have warned him, he thought. But he did not have much time for recriminations. Hardly had the growl died away before Pierrette choked back a scream in the darkness. Turning his head, Brandon saw the two wicked gleaming eyes of a jungle lion staring at them from deeper in the cave.

10

GRAVEYARD TO WHITE MAN

"LOOK OUT!" gasped Gaynor desperately.

"It's coming for us!" snapped Meyrick. "Stand back!"

The girl shrank against the low wall of the cave, her head bent, because there was not enough room to stand upright. Brandon took in the situation at a glance. He still gripped the revolver, but there was only one more shot left in its chambers and there was no time to reload with the few shells he still retained. Meyrick had the automatic, but that must be almost empty, too.

Then Gaynor shifted a little, thrusting a spear out in front of him as he crawled inwards to meet the slowly advancing lion. From the small amount of light that seeped in through the narrow entrance of the cave Brandon could see it was a big beast, full-maned and tawny in colour. From its slavering jaws deep rumbling snarls came at frequent intervals.

Brandon sized up the chances. He wormed his way past Pierrette and Meyrick, following Gaynor.

"Hold that spear tight," he muttered grimly. "When he comes at you jam the hilt against the floor. I'll fire at the same time."

"O.K." answered the pilot firmly.

"Tight spot, this," grunted Brandon. "Lion ahead and savages behind us!" He grinned in the darkness, excitement coursing through his veins like heady wine as the smell of battle teased his nostrils.

Gaynor said nothing, but fixed his eyes on the glowing stare of the on-coming lion. It crept towards them, as stealthy and cagey as any beast of the wild when cornered.

Then suddenly there was a deafening explosion near the mouth of the cave. Brandon flattened against the wall, thinking for an instant that Grier was firing his rifle in at the fugitives. But a shout from Meyrick brought his head round. Meyrick had fired the automatic pistol at one of the warriors who had at last located their whereabouts. All secrecy was gone. They were trapped between desperate men and a wild animal.

Startled into action by the crashing sound of the shot, the lion suddenly hurled itself forward in a spring that took it several yards. It bounded along the ground, snarling horribly as it bared its fangs. Gaynor rammed the hilt of his spear into the ground as he knelt full in the creature's path. The lion somehow or other missed the point of the weapon, knocking it aside with the force of its spring.

Gaynor was thrown sideways with a violence that banged his head against the rocky wall and partially stunned him. Brandon whipped clear just in time. With one hand he grabbed the spear shaft, twisting it round; with the other he fired the revolver straight into the lion's reeking jaws. The animal convulsed, stunned and blinded by the closeness of the explosion. From a great distance came a second report, as Meyrick fired again, outwards from cave mouth, keeping the attacking natives back as they sought to advance on the trapped men and the girl inside.

Then Brandon found the revolver dashed from his hand by the thrashing paws of the lion. Long raking claws tore at the flesh of his arm as he struggled to hold off the lion. Hot breath fanned at his face. Blood bubbled and gurgled in the creature's shattered throat. Brandon felt himself being forced over backwards by the compact weight and terrific vitality of the wounded animal.

With desperate strength he got his back against the wall of the low-roofed cave, bending forward grimly, wrenching the native spear up at an angle and driving its point into the lion's tawny body. Gaynor staggered clear of the fight, to reach out and worm past Brandon, making for Meyrick. With a grunt he seized Meyrick's automatic and returned to aid Brandon.

"Mind!" snapped Gaynor, bringing the automatic to bear.

Brandon, every muscle in his face and neck straining, grinned savagely.

"No need for that," he shot back. "Save the bullets for Grier and his buddies!"

Even as he spoke he relaxed. Before Gaynor's amazed eyes the body of the lion slowly sagged to the floor of the cave, dead and limp, its blood seeping from a deep wound in its side where Brandon had forced the spear right home to its heart.

Brandon examined his arm, which was bleeding freely from the raking claws of the king of the jungle. Gaynor started to say something, but Brandon brushed it aside as Meyrick shouted from close to the cave mouth. An instant later they realised something was happening. Gaynor turned and wriggled back through the confined space with the automatic, Brandon retrieved his revolver, feeling in his pocket for more ammunition. The smell of the dead lion was strong in his nostrils, but a faint breath of air came from deeper inside the cave. It was that which gave him a sudden idea. He passed Pierrette with a word of reassurance as the girl crouched on the floor.

"Meyrick," said Brandon. "We'll do better to carry on down this hole, I've a notion there's another opening in it somewhere."

"That should fox 'em!" grunted Meyrick. He peered through the cave mouth, smiling grimly to himself. "I got a couple of them," he added, thoughtfully. "There's no sign of Grier at the moment. Let's beat it while we have the chance!" He started creeping back from the entrance. The others followed as he and Brandon led the way further in, scrambling over the carcase of the lion where it barred their way. The going was difficult, for the cave grew progressively narrower and lower, so that before they had gone very far they were forced to crawl on their bellies.

Gaynor pushed the spear before him. Meyrick gripped the automatic and Brandon had his revolver. The floor of the cave was littered with dirt, old bones and bits of rotting flesh. To have walked right into a lion's den—quite literally—and got away with it was something Brandon had not done before.

There were moments during the nightmare journey through the cave when he did not think they would succeed in getting out of it. At one place Meyrick had great difficulty in thrusting his heavy body through the gap between the floor and the roof. Brandon had to turn and heave at his arms while Gaynor pushed from behind. Then, through the gloom ahead, they saw a small patch of light.

"We're getting somewhere," said Brandon grimly.

The cave, or tunnel, had been descending at a varying angle ever since they left its entrance after fighting the lion.

Pausing, Brandon listened intently, telling the others to be quiet. From far behind them, echoing strangely in the narrow confines of the cave, they could just hear the distant sound of voices and a scrambling noise as the warriors followed them quickly. Brandon guessed that Grier had urged them to enter the cave, for they would not have done so on their own initiative.

"They're after us," he muttered. "Come on; the sooner we get out of here and into the open the better."

Meyrick grunted full agreement as he crawled along in Brandon's wake. Pierrette came close behind him, with Jerry Gaynor bringing up the rear, glancing over his shoulder every now and again in the pitch blackness that closed in behind them. There was nothing to see.

Brandon had been trying to work out which direction the tunnel was taking, but it had turned and twisted several times since they entered it so that his task was more difficult than at first he thought it would be. However, he still had a vague idea of direction, despite the darkness. A fresh notion was buzzing round inside his head as he carried on. If it worked out to be correct—and events would quickly prove whether it was or not—they might find themselves considerably better off than they expected.

After another twenty or thirty yards of their crawling advance the patch of light ahead materialised into a rock-bound entrance to the tunnel.

"Wait!" breathed Brandon. He slithered forward on his own till he could peer through the hole. What he saw soon confirmed his previous ideas. The hole opened out in the side of a sheer, scrub-clad cliff. Below, ten or fifteen feet down, was the floor of what could only be the elephants' graveyard. Brandon took it in with satisfaction. As far as he could see the entire place was hemmed in by high walls, though there must, of course, be some other entrance to it in use by the dying elephants. The whole area was full of jungle growth, but here and there, through breaks in the foliage, he could see great piles of whitened bones and the long curving gleam of ivory tusks.

A whisper behind him brought Brandon's attention from the scene at which he stared in mute fascination.

"Hey, Rex, don't let me hurry you," said Meyrick, "but we can hear those damned savages coming up fast. I think Grier's with 'em. Hear a white man's voice."

"Right!" grunted Brandon. "Come on, then. We're entering the elephants' graveyard by the back door!" He eased himself through the hole in the cliffs, feeling with his toes for a hold in the scrub and lowering himself down.

Then Meyrick's bulky form appeared and wriggled through, to join him. Next came Pierrette, given a hand by Gaynor. Gaynor passed his spear down to Brandon and followed a moment later. They were all out of the cave now, standing on the floor of the deep depression that formed the graveyard.

"Rum sort of place, isn't it?" muttered Gaynor curiously. "I've never seen a spot like this in my life before."

"I doubt if you'll see another unless we get moving," said Brandon with sudden urgency. His gaze was fixed on the scrub and thorn some distance away. He thought he caught a glimpse of movement there. Instantly he was on the alert, for in a place like this anything could happen. A moment later it did.

"We have company," murmured Meyrick in a tight-lipped whisper. "This is an elephants' graveyard, isn't it? It looks as if we're disturbing one of the inmates."

Brandon shot him a glance that was full of meaning. Then he glanced over his shoulder hurriedly at a faint sound from the hole in the cliff face behind them. Grier, or the first of the warriors, was close to the entrance of the cave now. And then it was that a vast grey shape reared up from the cover of scrub and mchwrili trees where the movement had shown.

"This way!" snapped Brandon urgently. He started off at right-angles to where they were looking. But the old elephant scented and saw them. Dying though it might be, it resented this intrusion, and, game to the last, gave a shrill trumpet of anger as it launched itself in a thunderous charge.

Brandon was running fast, his companions close on his heels. He had no intention of tempting providence by facing a second charging elephant in the space of a few hours. There were things a man could get away with once, but not a second time. Discretion was better than being a fool, he decided. Then Meyrick gasped out something behind him. He turned and looked back, expected to see that Gaynor or the girl had gone down, or something of the kind. But what he saw made him halt abruptly with a soundless whistle on his pursed lips.

A shout from the mouth of the cave in the cliff reached his ears. He realised that Grier was jumping down to the floor of the graveyard. But what was more important was the fact that the dying elephant whose peace they had disturbed had sighted the newcomer. With less distance between Grier and itself, the beast was choosing the simpler victim.

Grier dropped to the ground, swinging round and bringing his rifle to bear on the charging elephant in one movement.

Brandon saw that the man was not armed with a heavy-bore gun. The bullet from it would have no more effect than a pea against the hide of the enraged animal.

"Run for it, Grier!" he yelled. "You're done if you don't!"

Either Grier did not hear, or chose to ignore him. The elephant crashed through the scrub, straight for the lone white man whose back was against the rocky wall of the place. With a furious trumpet of rage it bore in, the last of its waning strength going into the final effort.

Grier steadied his aim and fired. Once…twice… The bullets smacked into the on-coming beast. But they did not stop its rush. Grier left it too late to run. Before he fully realised what was coming he was caught by the great animal and smashed against the rocky wall behind him. His rifle flew through the air as the elephant's flailing trunk struck it from his hand.

Pierrette screamed in a helpless fashion as she saw what had happened. Jerry Gaynor's arm went round her shoulder.

Brandon, jaw set hard, wasted little sympathy on the man who had hounded them through the jungle. He was far more interested in their own possible fate when the elephant had finished with Grier. His eyes lit on the rifle where it lay about twenty yards distant. If he could get it, the odds would be considerably lessened.

Before any of his companions could prevent him he darted forward, grabbed up the rifle and levelled it just as the still-enraged elephant wheeled away from the crumpled form of Grier and stared round vindictively for further prey.

Seeing Brandon so near to it, it summoned the last of its failing strength and staggered towards him.

Brandon fired with the utmost care, aiming for the one vital spot presented to him. But hardly had he squeezed the trigger before the animal swayed and faltered. As his bullet burrowed through the tough hide the beast slowly toppled over sideways, dead before it hit the ground. The sudden exertion had over-taxed an already failing vitality. In spite of Brandon's shot it would never have reached him.

Brandon lowered the rifle, glanced up at the mouth of the tunnel in the cliff and caught sight of a native looking back at him. Then a spear whistled through the air. He drove himself sideways in the nick of time, firing Grier's rifle from his hip as he moved. There was a scream and the face of the warrior disappeared in the cave mouth.

Brandon stared hard at the cave for several seconds, but nothing else came in sight. Then he heard the voice of Pierrette. Looking away, he saw the girl running towards the battered body of Grier. Gaynor and Meyrick were close behind her, Meyrick calling out to her to be careful.

She dropped on one knee beside the crumpled-looking man, lifting his head on to her lap. "Uncle!" she said. "Uncle!"

Brandon thought he had better break up the party as soon as he could. They were in a dangerous position, and the sooner they left the vicinity of the cave mouth the better. His object was to secure a position from which he could cover the cave with Grier's rifle and so hold the attackers at bay should they attempt to enter the elephants' graveyard. Unless they took steps to do something concrete the place might well prove a graveyard for themselves. It looked as if it would be just that as far as Grier was concerned.

Striding towards the little group that had gathered round Grier's body, he pushed through and looked down at the man's blood-spattered face.

"Dead?" he inquired. He forced his voice to sound level out of deference to the girl's feelings. She looked up and met his gaze.

"No," she whispered in reply. There was a tell-tale moisture in her eyes. No matter what her uncle had been she felt his imminent death more deeply than she cared to admit.

"I'm sorry it had to happen that way, Pierrette," said Meyrick quietly and grimly. "He can't last, you know."

"I realise that," she muttered.

"We can't stay where we are," Brandon pointed out softly. He swivelled his gaze to the hole in the cliff.

"I won't leave him!" she insisted. "I—I can't; you must understand that. It wouldn't be human if I did."

"I didn't ask you to, Pierrette," he replied. "We must carry him with us to a better position. Before we know where we are those natives will be down here to wreak their revenge on us, don't forget."

She nodded dumbly. Meyrick and Gaynor lifted the broken body of Grier from the ground. Brandon relieved him of his cartridge belt and revolver, handing the latter to the girl. He also took Grier's hunting knife and stuck it in his own belt. Some good had come from the arrival of Grier.

Moving slowly and with many glances over their shoulders, the party left the vicinity of the dead elephant's carcase and the cave mouth in the cliff.

Brandon, who was bringing up the rear, kept a close eye on the cave mouth, his rifle at the ready. But he was a little puzzled when he saw no sign of the warriors. Surely, he thought, they would not have given up the chase so easily? They might be a superstitious lot, but the fact that their quarry was plainly in sight would have counteracted that. It was odd, to say the least.

They entered the undergrowth and halted, looking back. Brandon found Meyrick close beside him.

"What's the plan?" queried Meyrick.

"To find a second line of retreat," he replied. "And you can take another look at your white gold on the way!" He grinned cheerfully.

"There must be another entrance to this place—one the elephants use." As he spoke he threw a glance round, trying to follow the rim of the deep depression, searching for a break. The dense foliage made it difficult to see far enough.

Meyrick said: "What's happened to the natives? Why didn't they make another attack?"

Brandon was about to answer when Gaynor called urgently.

"They're coming at us now!" he cried. "From over there!"

11

TOUCH AND GO

"Tricked us!" said Meyrick in something like a snarl. "We've been watching the cave and all the time they were slipping back through it and working round to take us in the rear!"

Brandon made no reply; his eyes were darting this way and that, seeking to gain a full picture of their present position. The warriors, more than a score of them, were advancing cautiously through the scrub and trees. What Meyrick had said was right; they had come into the graveyard from another direction, and now it looked as if the little party would be caught in a dangerous trap.

"Too late to get back to the cliff!" snapped Brandon. "Best thing to do is fight our way through if we can."

Gaynor tightened his grip on Grier's revolver, which he had taken from Pierrette. Meyrick's jaw went out as he realised that their chances were not over-good. He glanced at Brandon. Brandon nodded curtly, levering a shell into his rifle with a click.

The warriors still came on, not fast, but steadily.

"All right!" said Brandon tersely. "Give it to 'em!"

The three men fired. Brandon brought down two of the attackers in quick succession. The range was long for Meyrick, but the bullets from their pistols must have passed unpleasantly close to the natives. Wails of dismay rent the air, mingled with cries of pain, as Brandon's shots went home with deadly effect.

The line of advancing warriors wavered and finally halted.

Brandon sprang upright, waving his arm to the others.

"Now!" he yelled. "As fast as you can!"

Pierrette, who was kneeling beside her uncle, gave a shuddering sigh. Grier had breathed his last just as Brandon called them. She rose to her feet, mouth tight. Jerry Gaynor grasped her by the arm, reading and guessing the things in her mind as he saw her face.

"Maybe it's better, Pierrette," he said as he hurried her forward at a run.

With Brandon leading the way, the four of them dashed at the thin line of natives. Several of them broke and ran in the face of the swift fire of pistols and rifle. A gap opened up in the line; but the warriors on either side of it were stiffening and preparing to meet the whites. Wild yells of hate and anger filled the peace of the graveyard. A throwing club caught Meyrick a glancing blow on the side of the head as he blundered along. It sent him reeling, but somehow or other he managed to recover. Brandon looked round, seeing his companions were still with him. Then he was horrified to see Gaynor stagger sideways and clutch at his arm. A lump of stone bounced to the ground, thrown by one of the nearest of the natives.

Pierrette cried out as she saw Gaynor stagger. Meyrick turned his head, cursing beneath his breath and firing twice.

Gaynor recovered his balance, but the check had given the attackers a chance to close in. Even as Gaynor changed his revolver from one hand to the other and started fighting again, several of the natives hurled themselves forward regardless of the death that struck at them as Brandon worked his rifle.

Meyrick was swearing softly as he plugged in a fresh clip of ammunition for the automatic. Pierrette was standing up straight, Grier's hunting knife gripped in her hand with desperate strength. One of the attackers launched himself directly at her, a club raised above his head to strike her down. Brandon saw the danger, whirled his rifle and fired. The bullet brought a scream of agony from the warrior. The descending club missed the girl's shoulder by a bare inch. Then Gaynor yelled urgently, his eyes fixed on a spot behind Brandon. Brandon whipped round in a flash. An enormous native was bearing down on him, spear up-lifted for a death blow. Brandon fired from the hip. There was a click as the pin fell dully on a spent cartridge. The rifle magazine was empty. Meyrick shouted to him, working feverishly to finish the loading of the automatic. Brandon clubbed the rifle and rushed at his enemy, yelling as loudly as any of the attackers themselves. The spear left the native's hand, sudden fear dawning in the man's face. Then Brandon's swinging rifle smashed his forehead with a sickening crunch. Brandon seized the spear where it stuck in the ground. Raising it, he hurled it at another of the attackers.

Meyrick, meanwhile, had reloaded his gun and was firing again. Gaynor, too, was once more a combatant force on his own. Pierrette stayed close at his side as they began to advance again. Their concentrated assault on the wild savages had gradually turned the tables. The natives were breaking once more, their numbers greatly reduced. But the danger was by no means over. Brandon knew they had a long way to go before they could hope to escape from the graveyard. And there might well be more of the natives in the vicinity.

Forcing the remaining warriors to fall back as they thrust their way forward, Brandon's party saved their ammunition as much as they could. Running fast, pursued by the warriors, they kept them out of spear range by occasional shots.

Brandon led them straight across the deep depression of the scrub-choked graveyard. On the way, they passed great mounds of whitened bones and yellowed ivory. The whole place was a veritable treasure-house of white gold. Even under the trying circumstances of their passage through it Meyrick found time to remark enthusiastically on the find.

Brandon compressed his lips, thinking that they would be lucky if they had another chance of viewing the graveyard. Instinct warned him that even when they reached the entrance of the place there would be danger awaiting them.

He was not even sure whereabouts the entrance would be, but was working entirely from common-sense, based on the line of attack used by the warriors.

Panting and weary, the fugitives plunged on through the scrub and thorn, their clothes almost ripped from their bodies by the vicious hooks and claws of the foliage.

Suddenly Meyrick gave a grunt of satisfaction.

"Over there!" he gasped. "Look, there's a break in the rimrock and a slope leading upwards. That's our line!"

Brandon nodded without speaking. He turned aside a little, heading straight for the break. A clean slope of smoothed rock formed a natural roadway into the graveyard. Trees and scrub grew thickly on either side of the slope, narrowing it down considerably. But for all that it now represented a way of escape for the hard-pressed whites.

The natives were still following them as closely as they dared, but sporadic shooting forced them to keep their distance.

Brandon forced the pace even more, knowing that the more ground they gained the better would be the chances. He knew, that in a straight run the natives would outstrip them, but if once they were able to use their own bush-craft, the odds would be less.

They were half-way up the steep rocky slope when he looked up and saw something that brought a curse to his lips.

"My God!" gasped Meyrick chokingly, behind him. "More of the devils! This is our end!"

Spreading across the top of the slope in a madly-dancing line were the gesticulating figures of thirty or more of the hostile natives. They were obviously reinforcements for the party already in the graveyard, and Brandon began to realise why their first enemies had not hurled themselves in for the kill during the retreat. Instead, they had merely acted as a spur to the whites, driving them deeper into the trap already prepared.

Brandon gritted his teeth and levelled his rifle with a desperate calm. If they were to be caught in a trap of this kind they would go down fighting to the last. It was plain that Meyrick and Gaynor were of the same mind, for they pressed close to Brandon's side and used their own guns to good effect.

But the numbers against them were large. More and more of the natives appeared from either side of the rocky slope, adding to the odds against them.

To make matters worse, the natives behind them took extra courage when they sighted their comrades. Harried from front and rear, Brandon and his three companions knew, in their hearts, that the end must come unless a miracle happened.

Waves of warriors were rushing at them from the top of the slope. The handful that remained below were thrusting up at them. Ammunition was running dangerously low, and it was certain that they did not have sufficient cartridges left between them to kill half the numbers hurled against them.

"Make the most of it, everyone!" shouted Meyrick. He was sweating profusely, but there was a grin on his face as he yelled out and dodged a spear, firing as he moved. There was a scream of rage and pain from somewhere in the bush.

"Break for the jungle!" called Brandon. He fired his rifle again, then led the way to the edge of the slope where the trees would offer some cover.

Pierrette staggered after him. There was blood on her cheek and one of her arms hung limply at her side. But she still gripped the hunting knife and her eyes were alight with a grim determination. Gaynor had the use of only one arm, for the stone that had struck him previously had almost broken the bone. Meyrick was dizzy from a crack on the head, and Brandon alone remained unscathed. Even he was suffering from various minor wounds inflicted during his fight with the lion and the dying elephant.

They ducked through the outer fringe of undergrowth, but barely had they done so before Brandon stiffened as he caught a glimpse of movement ahead.

Three or more of the natives sprang towards him, brandishing spears in their hands. He cut down one of them with the rifle. Meyrick used another bullet to deal with the second, but the third of the trio broke through and reached them, yelling and throwing the spear straight at Gaynor. Gaynor dashed himself aside, taking Pierrette with him as he fell. The spear missed his chest by a narrow margin, but buried itself in his upper arm, bringing a cry of pain from his lips.

Brandon knew that they were done for now. With Gaynor wounded they could not hope to break out. It was only a matter of time before they were overwhelmed and slaughtered, or captured, for sacrifice by the Elephant God people.

Teeth bared in a vicious snarl, he turned and smashed at the native with his rifle, using it club-fashion, rather than spend another shot at such close range. The rifle crunched on bone and flesh. Then more of the warriors were coming in from the slope, surrounding the fugitives as they closed in.

"This looks like it, Rex!" grunted Meyrick grimly. "I'm damned sorry to have brought you into this. My fault."

"Forget it!" snapped Brandon. He crouched like a wild animal, waiting for the final assault to be launched. If he and his friends were to die they would take as many of their attackers with them as they could.

All four of them were kneeling now. Other natives were breaking noisily through the undergrowth to take them in the rear. The whites formed a square, determined to fight back-to-back to the last.

"Wait for it!" grunted Gaynor. "They're massing now. I can see them."

Brandon strained his ears. Meyrick was breathing hard at his side. Pierrette suddenly sobbed uncontrollably at his back, where she crouched beside Gaynor. There was a long silence that seemed to drag on interminably. Then the crackle of breaking thorn reached their ears.

"Last stand!" muttered Brandon. He spoke more to himself than to anyone else.

But suddenly and unexpectedly there was another sound in the jungle around them. It grew gradually louder and louder, a deep throb, rising and falling in a slow cadence that was music to the besieged white men.

"My plane!" whispered Gaynor incredulously. "Listen; it's coming this way!"

The natives appeared to be listening, too, for there was no further sound from their direction. Brandon caught a glimpse of alarmed faces peering round as the throb of the motor came closer.

"This may be our chance!" breathed Brandon tensely. "If it is, we shall have to snatch it and run like the devil. Can you make it, Jerry?"

"Think so," came the reply.

The throb of the aircraft had risen to a roar now. It was circling the graveyard swiftly, searching, it seemed.

Brandon held his breath. Then he leapt to his feet with a yell of triumph. The deafening roar of the plane was having its effect on the natives. With one accord they lost their nerve and scattered, crashing through the scrub in wild haste to escape from the terror that circled in the sky above their heads. They broke and fled before the sound and the bird-like shadow. And Brandon and his companions hurried them on their way with several shots as they struck out and gained the slope again.

"Come on!" rapped Brandon, urging the others forward. He kept an eye on Gaynor, but the pilot seemed to be getting along well enough with the help of Pierrette. Sprinting for the top of the slope, Brandon paused and stared up at the plane. There could be little doubt as to who was piloting it. Darracq, defeated once, had returned to camp and taken to the air.

"First useful thing he's ever done," grunted Meyrick. "Saved our bacon that time, didn't he?"

Brandon began to grin as the aircraft dipped and headed for them. Then the growing smile suddenly left his face. The plane was almost overhead, flying low. The cabin window opened, revealing Darracq's face as he peered down at them. His hand showed through the window. Something egg-shaped was gripped in the fingers.

"No!" yelled Meyrick. "No, he can't do that! It's a bomb!"

Brandon stared round grimly. "Down!" he yelled.

They flung themselves flat on their faces. The plane roared low over their heads. Brandon raised his eyes for an instant, expecting the crash of the explosion at any moment.

Then suddenly Gaynor whistled unbelievingly. Brandon saw the reason an instant later. Darracq threw the grenade downwards, but they saw it caught and held in the bottom of the double wing-strut. Next moment there was a blinding flash. The aircraft staggered, bursting into flames fifty feet above the ground. It dropped like a stone, sheets of flame enveloping the fuselage as it crashed.

Brandon got to his feet, conscious of wonder at the manner of their reprieve. He looked round swiftly, taking his eyes from the funeral pyre of Darracq and meeting the gaze of his three companions.

"That's that," he said briefly. "We'd better be on our way before the natives pluck up courage again and come back to finish us off!"

Choosing a path that was screened by the billowing clouds of smoke that rose from the still-burning aircraft, Brandon set off. Gaynor cast a rueful glance at his plane, but he made no complaint about its loss. Pierrette was silent as she strode along at his side. Meyrick shrugged his broad shoulders as he turned his back on the treasure of white gold they were leaving behind. Brandon read his thoughts.

"We'll come back another time," he said. "Our main object now is to reach the vehicles and get out of here!"

Meyrick grunted cheerfully enough. "Of course," he said. "We might take another partner with us next time."

Brandon shot him a glance. "Meaning…?"

Meyrick turned and looked at Gaynor. "Jerry," he said. "We can't pay for your plane, but we like you. Will you join us in another safari later on? Share of the ivory as payment for the plane."

Gaynor grinned happily. "Nothing would suit me better!" he returned. "Unless…"

"Come by all means," cut in Pierrette with a smile. "I might even join you myself—if Rex will let me!"

Brandon hid a smile. "You mean if Jerry will let you, don't you?" he teased. "We'll see about it. Come on, all of you. We've still got a long way to trek."

Content, despite the dangers that still beset their path, the four of them set off briskly through the jungle. No one spoke for a long time, till suddenly Brandon halted and held up his hand. Peering at the ground, he dropped to one knee and examined some barely visible tracks.

"Someone has been this way recently," he muttered grimly.

Meyrick grunted and mopped his forehead. The heat was oppressive. Then he stiffened as a sound reached their ears from the undergrowth ahead. Brandon brought his rifle to the ready, peering forward. The thorn bushes parted and a stealthy figure emerged, head going from side to side as it searched the surroundings cautiously.

Brandon relaxed an instant later. "Llanga, by all that's holy!" he gasped in amazement. "Hey, Llanga, here we are!"

His shout brought the Shangaan running towards them. In his wake game two more of Meyrick's bearers. They were all who remained alive of the original safari party. The reunion was mutually pleasant, and Brandon was delighted to have some extra men for the return journey.

Once again they set off; this time with lighter hearts than ever. Further adventure lay ahead, but none of them shirked the prospect. The lure of white gold would bring them back, as surely as it had led them through the forest in the first place.

THE END

DENIS HUGHES

DENIS (TALBOT) HUGHES (1917-2008)

BORN in London, England, Hughes was the son of noted Victorian artist Talbot Hughes. He was training as a pilot during WW2, when a serious crash ended his flying career. Attracted to writing by the expanding post-war market in paperback publishing, his first book (an espionage thriller) was published in 1948.

Over the next six years, an astonishing more than 80 novels followed, chiefly westerns and science fiction, with a dozen jungle-adventure novels.

In 1950, his UK publisher Curtis Warren had launched their six-novel *Azan the Apeman* series, written by "Marco Garron" (David Griffiths), commissioned after the hugely successful Mark Goulden/W. H. Allen (later Pinnacle Books) reprints of ERB's Tarzan novels.

But the 'Azan the Apeman' banner was such a blatant copy of Tarzan that E.R.B. Inc. threatened Curtis with prosecution unless the books were taken off the market.

To cover their losses, in May 1951 Curtis Warren brought Denis Hughes into the writing seat and a new series of jungle adventures began, this time featuring his original character, Rex Brandon. To capitalize on their earlier series, Curtis Warren issued the books under the byline of

'Marco Garon' (only one 'r' in 'Garon').

These fast-moving action-packed novels books were successful enough for the publisher and author to issue a further six titles in 1951, and another four in 1952. Most of these short novels have decidedly fantastic elements, and are infused with the same weird imagination Hughes displayed in his many 'science fantasy' novels. All of them are set in the African jungle, except for the last one, Mountain Gold, which, exceptionally, is a 'straight' adventure set in the Yukon.

When his main publisher collapsed in 1954, Hughes switched to writing exclusively for the established D.C. Thomson, famous publisher of boys' papers. Until his retirement in the 1980s Hughes became one of their mainstay (albeit anonymous) writers for such comics as Victor, Hotspur, Wizard and Warlord (the latter title inspired by Hughes' "Scarlet Pimpernel" type WW2 secret agent character, Lord Peter Flint, alias 'Warlord'.)

Because most of his novels had been published pseudonymously, Hughes fell out of print for many years, until researcher Philip Harbottle revealed his authorship. Since then all of his 'lost' novels are currently being reprinted under his real name.

"FANS OF TARZAN AND DOC SAVAGE WILL FEEL RIGHT AT HOME WITH REX BRANDON"
— PAPERBACKWARRIOR.COM

1 THE ADVENTURES OF REX BRANDON, JUNGLE HUNTER BY DENIS HUGHES

DEATH WARRIORS
REX BRANDON
JUNGLE HUNTER

2 THE ADVENTURES OF REX BRANDON, JUNGLE HUNTER BY DENIS HUGHES

JUNGLE ALLIES
REX BRANDON
JUNGLE HUNTER

Published through arrangement with Cosmos Literary Agency.

WWW.BOLDVENTUREPRESS.COM

REX BRANDON: JUNGLE HUNTER TM & © 2024 The Estate of Denis Hiughes. All rights reserved.

An iron-fisted ex-Confederate sergeant ...
A gun-slinging ex-Union captain...
Destiny paired them to hunt for a fortune in gold ...
To pursue the thief ... To brave a thousand perils!

BENEDICT AND BRAZOS

by E. JEFFERSON CLAY

"Aces Wild [#1] is a really entertaining traditional Western with a pair of likable protagonists ... I'll be reading more of them, you can count on that. Recommended."

James Reasoner, *Rough Edges*

WWW.BOLDVENTUREPRESS.COM

Benedict And Brazos
TM & © 2024
Piccadilly Publishing.
All Rights Reserved.

His gun is for hire when the job and the money are right.

O'BRIEN™

— BEN BRIDGES —

WWW.BOLDVENTUREPRESS.COM

O'BRIEN TM & © 2024 Ben Bridges. All Rights Reserved.

AUSTLIT

The definitive resource for Australian literature

A research environment for Australian literary, print, and narrative cultures ...

AustLit is a searchable, scholarly source of information about Australian writers and writing, documenting more than 200 years of publishers, newspapers, magazines and scholarly journals. Learn more at

https://www.austlit.edu.au/

AustLit is brought to you by The University of Queensland in collaboration with academic, library, education and research organisations.

THE UNIVERSITY OF QUEENSLAND
AUSTRALIA